A. Carter

HEIST SOCIETY

Also by Ally Carter

Ally Carter

HEIST SOCIETY

ORCHARD

ORCHARD BOOKS
First published in The United States in 2010
by Hyperion Books for Children
This edition published in 2018 by The Watts Publishing Group

1 3 5 7 9 10 8 6 4 2

A CIP catalogue record for this book is available from the British Library.

ISBN 978 1 40834 999 1

Printed and Bound by CPI Group (UK) Ltd, Croydon, CR0 4YY

The paper and board used in this book are made from wood
from responsible sources.

MIX
Paper from
responsible sources
FSC® C104740

Orchard Books
An imprint of Hachette Children's Group
Part of The Watts Publishing Group Limited
Carmelite House
50 Victoria Embankment
London EC4Y 0DZ
An Hachette UK Company
www.hachette.co.uk

www.hachettechildrens.co.uk

For my family

ONE

No one knew for certain when the trouble started at the Colgan School. Some members of its alumni association blamed the decision to admit girls. Others cited newfangled liberal ideals and a general decline in the respect for elders worldwide. But whatever the theory, no one could deny that, recently, life at the Colgan School was different.

Oh, its grounds were still perfectly manicured. Three quarters of the senior class were already well on their way to being early-accepted into the Ivy League. Photos of presidents and senators and CEOs still lined the dark-panelled hallway outside the headmaster's office.

But in the old days, no one would ever have declined admission to Colgan on the day before classes started, forcing the administration to scramble to fill the slot. Historically, any vacancy would have been met with a waiting list a mile long, but this year, for some reason, there was only one applicant eager to enrol at that late date.

Most of all, there had been a time when honour meant something at the Colgan School, when school property was respected, when the faculty was revered – when the head-master's mint-condition 1958 Porsche Speedster would *never* have been placed on top of the fountain in the quad with water shooting out of its headlights on an unusually warm evening in November.

There had been a time when the girl responsible – the very one who had lucked into that last-minute vacancy only a few months before – would have had the decency to admit what she'd done and quietly taken her leave of the school. But unfortunately, that era, much like the headmaster's car, was finished.

Two days after Porsche-gate, as the students had taken to calling it, the girl in question had the nerve to sit in the hallway of the administration building beneath the black-and-white stare of three senators, two presidents, and a Supreme Court justice, with her head held high, as if she'd done nothing wrong.

More students than usual filed down the corridor that day, going out of their way to steal a glance and whisper behind cupped hands.

"That's her."

"She's the one I was telling you about."

"How do you think she did it?"

Any other student might have flinched in that bright spotlight, but from the moment Katarina Bishop set foot on the Colgan campus, she'd been something of an enigma. Some said she'd gained her last-minute slot because she was the daughter of an incredibly wealthy European businessman who had made a very generous donation. Some looked at her perfect posture and cool demeanour, rolled her first name across their tongues, and assumed that she was Russian royalty – one of the last of the Romanovs.

Some called her a hero; others called her a freak.

Everyone had heard a different story, but no one knew the truth – that Kat really had grown up all over Europe, but she wasn't an heiress. That she did, in fact, have a Fabergé egg, but she wasn't a Romanov. Kat herself could have added a thousand rumours to the mill, but she stayed quiet, knowing that the only thing no one would believe was the truth.

"Katarina?" the headmaster's secretary called. "The board will see you now."

Kat rose calmly, but as she stepped towards the open door twenty feet from the headmaster's office, she heard her shoes squeak; she felt her hands tingle. Every nerve in her body seemed to stand on end as she realized that somehow, in the last three months, she had become someone who wore squeaky shoes.

That, whether she liked it or not, they were going to hear her coming.

Kat was used to looking at a room and seeing all the angles, but she'd never seen a room quite like this before.

Though the hallway outside was long and straight, this room was round. Dark wood surrounded her; dim lights hung from a low ceiling. It felt to Kat almost like a cave, except for a tall, slim window where a narrow beam of sunlight came pouring in. Suddenly, Kat found herself reaching out, wanting to run her hands through the rays. But then someone cleared his throat, a pencil rolled across a desk, and Kat's shoes squeaked again, bringing her back to the moment.

"You may sit down."

The voice came from the back of the room, and at first Kat didn't know who'd spoken. Like the voice, the faces before her were unfamiliar: the twelve on her right were wrinkle-free and fresh – students just like her (or as much like her as a Colgan student could possibly be). The twelve people on her left had hair that was a little thinner, or makeup that was a little heavier. But regardless of age, all the members of the Colgan School Honour Board were wearing identical black robes and impassive expressions as they watched Kat walk to the centre of the circular room.

"Sit, Ms Bishop," Headmaster Franklin said from his place in the front row. He looked especially pale in his dark robe. His cheeks were too puffy, his hair too styled. He was the sort of man, Kat realized, who probably wished he were as fast and sporty as his car. And then, despite everything, Kat grinned a little, imagining the headmaster himself propped up in the middle of the quad, squirting water.

As Kat took her seat, the senior boy beside the headmaster rose and announced, "The Colgan School Honour Board shall come to order." His voice echoed around the room. "All who wish to speak shall be heard. All who wish to follow the light shall see. All who wish to seek justice shall find the truth. Honour for one," the boy finished, and before Kat could really process what she'd heard, twenty-four voices chorused, "Honour for all."

The boy sat and ruffled through the pages of an old leather-bound book until the headmaster prodded, "Jason…"

"Oh. Yeah." Jason picked up the heavy book. "The Colgan School Honour Board will hear the case of Katarina Bishop, sophomore. The committee will hear testimony that on the tenth of November, Ms Bishop did willfuly …um…*steal* personal property." Jason chose his words carefully, while a girl in the second row stifled a laugh.

"That by committing this act at two am, she was also in violation of the school curfew. And that Ms Bishop wilfully destroyed school artifacts." Jason lowered the book and paused – a little more dramatically than necessary, Kat thought – before he added, "According to the Colgan Code of Honour, these charges are punishable by expulsion. Do you understand the charges as they have been read to you?"

Kat took a moment to make sure the board really did want her to respond before she said, "I didn't do it."

"The charges." Headmaster Franklin leaned forward. "The question, Ms Bishop, was whether you *understood* the charges."

"I do." Kat felt her heartbeat change rhythm. "I just don't agree with them."

"I—" the headmaster started again, but a woman to his right touched his arm lightly.

She smiled at Kat as she said, "Headmaster, I seem to remember that in matters such as this, it's customary to take the student's full academic history into account. Perhaps we should begin with a review of Ms Bishop's record?"

"Oh." The headmaster seemed to deflate a bit. "Well, that's quite right, Ms Connors, but since Ms Bishop has only been with us a few months, she has no record to speak of."

"But surely this is not the first school the young woman has attended?" Ms Connors asked, and Kat bit back a nervous laugh.

"Well, yes," the headmaster admitted grudgingly. "Of course. And we tried to contact those schools, but there was a fire at Trinity that destroyed the entire admissions office and most of their records. And the Bern Institute experienced a terrible computer crash last summer, so we've had a very difficult time finding...things."

The headmaster looked at Kat as if disasters must follow wherever she went. Ms Connors, on the other hand, looked impressed. "Those are two of the finest schools in Europe."

"Yes, ma'am. My father, he...does a lot of work there."

"What *do* your parents do?"

As Kat searched the second row for the girl who'd posed the question, she started to ask exactly why her parents' occupations mattered. But then she remembered that Colgan was the kind of place where who your parents were and what they did always seemed to matter.

"My mother died when I was six."

A few people gave a slight sigh at this, but Headmaster Franklin pressed on. "And your father?" he asked, unwilling to let a conveniently deceased mother swing any sympathy votes Kat's way. "What does *he* do?"

"Art," Kat said simply, carefully. "He does a lot of things, but he specializes in art."

At this, the head of the fine arts department perked up. "Collecting?" the man asked.

Again Kat had to fight back a smile. "More like… *distribution*."

"Interesting though this may be," Headmaster Franklin interrupted, "it does not pertain to…the matter at hand." Kat could have sworn he'd stopped himself from saying *to my convertible*.

No one responded. The only motion in the room was the dust that still danced in the narrow beam of falling light. Finally, Headmaster Franklin leaned forwards and narrowed his eyes. Kat had seen lasers with less focus as the headmaster snapped: "Ms Bishop, where were you on the night of November tenth?"

"In my room. Studying."

"On a Friday night? You were studying?" The headmaster glanced at his colleagues as if that were the most outrageous lie any Colgan student had ever dared to utter.

"Well, Colgan *is* an exceptionally difficult institution. I have to study."

"And you didn't see anyone?" Jason asked.

"No, I—"

"Oh, but someone saw *you*, didn't they, Ms Bishop?" Headmaster Franklin's voice was cold and sharp. "We have cameras monitoring the grounds. Or didn't you know?" he asked with a chuckle.

But of course Kat knew about the cameras. She suspected she knew more about every aspect of Colgan security than the headmaster did, but she didn't think this was the appropriate time to say so. There were too many witnesses. Too much was at stake. And, besides, the headmaster was already smiling triumphantly and dimming the lights with a remote control. Kat had to twist in her chair to see a section of the round wall sliding aside, revealing a large TV.

"This young woman bears a striking resemblance to you, does she not, Ms Bishop?" As Kat watched the grainy black-and-white video, she recognized the quad, of course, but she had never seen the person who was running across it wearing a black hooded sweatshirt.

"That's not me."

"But the dormitory doors were only opened once that night – at 2:27 am – using a student identification card. *This* card." Kat's stomach flipped as the single-worst picture she had ever taken appeared on the screen. "This is your Colgan student ID, is it not, Ms Bishop?"

"Yes, but—"

"And this" – Headmaster Franklin reached beneath his seat – "was found during a search of your belongings." The personalized licence plate – COLGAN-1 – seemed to glow as he held it above his head.

It felt to Kat as though all the air had left the dim room as a strange feeling swept over her. After all, *accused* she could handle; *wrongly accused* was entirely new territory.

"Katarina?" Ms Connors asked, as if begging Kat to prove them wrong.

"I know that *seems* like a lot of very convincing evidence," Kat said, her mind working, gears spinning. "Maybe too much evidence? I mean, would I really use my own ID if I'd done it?"

"So since there is evidence that you *did* it, that should prove that you *didn't* do it?" Even Ms Connors sounded sceptical.

"Well," Kat said, "I'm not stupid."

The headmaster laughed. "Oh, well, how would *you* have done it?" He was mocking her – baiting her – yet Kat couldn't help but think about the answer:

There was a shortcut behind Warren Hall that was closer and darker and completely void of cameras...

The doors wouldn't need an ID. to open if you had enough Bubblicious to cover the sensor on your way out...

If you're going to pull a prank of that nature, you don't do

it the night before a morning when the maintenance staff will
be awake long before the students...

Headmaster Franklin smiled smugly, relishing her silence, as if he were so smart.

But Kat had already learned that people at Colgan were frequently wrong – like when her Italian teacher had said that Kat's accent would always make her stand out on the streets of Rome (even though Kat had already passed for a Franciscan nun during a particularly difficult job in Vatican City). She thought about how silly her History of Art teacher had sounded when she'd waxed poetic about seeing the *Mona Lisa* (when Kat knew for a fact that the Louvre's original had been replaced with a fake in 1862).

Kat had learned quite a lot of things before enrolling at the Colgan School – but the thing that she knew best was that this was the kind of place where she could never share them.

"I don't know about Trinity or Bern or any of those *European* schools, young lady, but at the Colgan School we follow the rules." The headmaster's fist banged the table. "We respect the property of others. We adhere to the honour code of this institution and the laws of this country."

But Kat already knew about honour. She'd grown up

with her own set of rules. And the first rule of Katarina Bishop's family was simple: Don't get caught.

"Katarina," Ms Connors said, "do you have anything to add that might explain this?"

Kat could have said, *That's not me* or *There must be some kind of mistake*. The great irony was that if this had been an ordinary con, she could have lied her way through it without a second thought. But the truth? That, she wasn't so good at.

Her ID. badge had been duplicated. The licence plate had been planted in her room. Someone had dressed like her and made sure they were caught on camera.

She'd been framed. And Kat didn't dare say what she was thinking: that whoever had done it, they were very, very good.

Kat's bags were packed in twenty minutes. She might have lingered, saying her goodbyes, but there were no goodbyes to say. And so, after three months at Colgan, Kat couldn't help but wonder if the day she got expelled from boarding school might become the proudest moment of her family's long and colourful past. She imagined everyone sitting around Uncle Eddie's kitchen table years from now, telling about the time little Katarina stole a whole other life and then walked away without a trace.

Well, almost, Kat thought as she carried her bags past the once-perfect lawn. Ruts still tracked to and from the mangled fountain in the centre of the quad: a muddy reminder that would no doubt last until spring.

She heard laughter coming from behind her, and turned. A group of eighth grade boys was standing together, whispering, until one bravely broke away from the pack.

"Uh…" he started, then glanced back at his friends, summoning courage. "We were wondering…um. How'd you do it?"

A stretch limo pulled through the ornate gates and up to the kerb. The boot popped open. As the driver started for her bags, Kat looked at the boys and then back at Colgan one final time. "*That* is an excellent question."

The bells chimed. Students hurried between classes, across the quad. And as Kat crawled into the backseat of the limo, she couldn't help feeling slightly sad, or as sad as anyone could feel about losing something that wasn't rightfully theirs to begin with. She leaned back and sighed, "Well, I guess that's over."

And it would have been…if another voice hadn't said, "Actually, it's just beginning."

TWO

Kat jumped. In the dim light, she hadn't noticed the figure sitting at the other end of the limo's bench, smiling back at her.

"Hale?" she asked as if the boy might be an imposter. But then a very different question crossed her mind. "Hale, what are you doing here?"

"I thought you might need a ride."

"The headmaster's office called me a car."

He shrugged, indifferent but amused. "And here I am in a submarine."

As the limo pulled out of the school's circular driveway, Hale turned and looked out the window. Kat watched him take in the grounds, a faint smile on his lips as if there were no place on earth he really had to be. Kat sometimes wondered if that kind of self-assurance was something only very old money could buy. Then she wondered if it was something you could steal.

Hale waved as the gates of the Colgan School faded into the distance. "Goodbye, Colgan!" He turned to her. "Hello, Kitty Kat."

"Hale, how did you know I was..."

But Kat didn't finish. Suddenly, she wasn't in the back of a limo – she was sitting on a hard chair, staring at the black-and-white surveillance footage of someone in a hooded sweatshirt running across the quad. She was looking at the image of her own student ID. magnified on a TV screen. She was watching Headmaster Franklin hold a crumpled vanity plate above his head for all to see.

"Hale," Kat sighed. "The headmaster's car? Really? That's not too clichéd for you?"

"What can I say?" He shrugged. "I'm an old-fashioned guy. Besides, it's a classic for a reason." He leaned against the window. "It's good to see you, Kat."

Kat didn't know what to say. It's good to see you too? Thanks for getting me kicked out? Is it possible you've got even hotter? I think I might have missed you?

So instead she settled on, "Did my father put you up to this?"

Hale exhaled a quick laugh and shook his head. "He hasn't treturned my calls since Barcelona." He leaned closer and whispered, "I think he might still be mad at me."

"Yeah, well, that makes two of us."

"Hey," Hale snapped. "We all agreed that that monkey seemed perfectly well trained at the time."

Kat simply shook her head. "You got me kicked out, Hale."

He grinned and gave a slow bow. "You're welcome."

"You trashed the headmaster's car."

"W. W. Hale the Fourth bought that car *for* Headmaster Franklin, or didn't they mention that? Granted, it was to make up for a fire that W. W. Hale the Fifth *allegedly* started in the eighth grade – before they suggested that all current and future W. W. Hales continue their educations elsewhere – which worked out just as well since I'm at the Knightsbury Institute now."

"I've never heard of it."

"My father got a letter just last week telling him that I have become a model student."

"Congratulations," Kat said, doubting it.

"Yeah, well, I'm the only student." He grinned a very Hale-like grin. "Of course, the downside of attending a fictional school is that our lacrosse team sucks. Anyway, if the Colgan School wanted to be technical about it, I trashed *my* car."

She studied W. W. Hale the Fifth. He looked older than sixteen, with messy light brown hair and golden skin, and a first name that, despite two years of effort,

Kat had never learned.

"I doubt they'd see it that way, *Wesley*?" she guessed.

Hale smiled. "Not. Even. Close."

So far Kat had been through all the Wa's she could think of, but Hale hadn't admitted to being Walter or Ward or Washington. He'd firmly denied both Warren and Waverly. Watson had prompted him to do a very bad Sherlock Holmes impersonation throughout a good portion of a train ride to Edinburgh, Scotland. And Wayne seemed so wrong that she hadn't even tried.

Hale was Hale. And not knowing what the W's stood for had become a constant reminder to Kat that, in life, there are some things that can be given but never stolen.

Of course, that didn't stop her from trying.

"So, how long before you broke into the student records office?" Hale asked. "A week?" Kat felt her cheeks go red. "But you didn't find anything on me, did you?" He raised an eyebrow. "Kat," he sighed her name. "That is so sweet. And innocent. Naive looks good on you."

"Don't get used to it."

He shook his head. "Oh, I won't."

The whisperlike purr of the engine filled the car as it snaked through the countryside.

"Why'd you do it, Hale?"

"You don't belong in that place."

"Why'd you do it?" she asked again, her patience wearing thin. "I'm not joking, Hale."

"Neither am I, Kat."

"You've got—"

"A job for you," Hale said. "And *only* you," he added before she could protest.

The hills were growing steeper. Leaves scattered in the wind, and in the distance, the sun glistened off a lake. But Kat didn't take her eyes off Hale as she said, "I don't *want* a job."

"You'll want this one."

"I'm out of the family business. Or haven't you heard?"

"Fine." Hale crossed his arms and sank deeper into the seat. He leaned his head back and closed his eyes. Kat could have sworn he was already half asleep when he asked, "But are you out of the family?"

THREE

Of all the houses the Hale family owned, W. W. Hale the Fifth's favourite wasn't the penthouse on Park Avenue (too pretentious), or the flat in Hong Kong (too noisy), or even the mansion on Martha's Vineyard (entirely too much sand). No, the youngest Hale was only truly fond of the old, six-hundred-acre estate in rural New York. At least, that was the only place where Kat had ever heard him say…

"We're home."

The foyer was two storeys tall and stretched in front of them for at least thirty feet. Hale walked ahead of her, hurrying past the Monet in the hall as if that would keep her from noticing it – or stealing it. He gestured toward the stairs. "Marcus put you in the blue room. You can go upstairs if you want. Or we can go out to the veranda and have Marcus bring you something to eat. Are you hungry? I didn't even ask. Do you want—"

"I want you to tell me what's going on."

After hours of watching the New England countryside roll by, and listening to Hale snore, Kat was finished with plotting and strategizing how to get her boarding school life back. She was out of options, so she called upon every thief's oldest and most trusted method for getting what she wants: Ask nicely.

"Please, Hale."

But he didn't answer. He was too busy walking down the main hall, guiding Kat into a dim room that she had never seen before. Moonlight cascaded through the windows that lined one wall. There were bookshelves and leather sofas, brandy decanters and the stale smell of old cigars and even older money. There was no doubt in Kat's mind that it was an important room. For important men. And yet Kat brushed past Hale without a second thought...until she saw the painting.

Stepping towards it was like approaching a window into another country, another century. She studied the rich colours and strong brushstrokes. "It's beautiful," she whispered, staring at the work of an Old Master in the moonlight.

"It's Vermeer."

Kat turned to the boy who lingered in the doorway. "It's stolen."

"What can I say?" Hale eased behind her and studied the painting over her shoulder. "I met a very nice man who bet me that he had the best security system in Istanbul." His breath was warm on the back of her neck. "He was mistaken."

Kat stayed perfectly still as Hale walked to the desk in the far corner of the massive room, picked up a telephone and said, "Marcus, we're home. Could you get some – Yeah. The library." He held his hand over the receiver. "Do you like corned beef?" Kat glared at him, but he only smiled. "She loves it!" he exclaimed. He hung up and collapsed onto one of the leather sofas as if he owned the place, which, Kat had to remind herself, he did.

"So," Hale said with a slow, easy grin, "did you miss me?"

A good thief is always a great liar. It's part of the skill set, the tools, the craft. And at that moment, Kat thought it was probably a very good thing she'd walked away from the life, because when she said, "No," Hale just smiled wider.

"It really is good to see you, Kat."

"You might want to remember who I am before you try to con me."

"No." Hale shook his head. "*You* might want to remember who you are. You want to go back to Colgan, is that it? After I saved you from that place?"

"Colgan wasn't so bad. I could have been normal at Colgan."

Hale laughed. "Trust me: *you* would never have been normal at Colgan."

"I could have been *happy* at Colgan."

"They kicked you out, Kat."

"Because *you* framed me!"

Hale shrugged. "Fair enough." He stretched his arms over the back of the couch. "I sprung you because I've got a message for you."

"Doesn't your family own a cell phone company?"

"Only a little one." He held his fingers an inch apart to illustrate his point. "Besides, it's more of a face-to-face kind of message."

"I thought my dad wasn't speaking to..." She trailed off. Hale shook his head. And suddenly Kat understood everything a little better. She dropped onto the sofa opposite him and asked, "So how is Uncle Eddie?"

"He's good." Hale nodded. "He sends his love. He says the Colgan School will rob you of your soul." She started to protest, but Hale stopped her. "But that's not the message."

"Hale," Kat exhaled, growing weary.

"Kat," Hale mimicked. "Do you want to hear Uncle Eddie's message or not?"

"Yes."

"He says he's got to give them back."

"What?" Kat was sure she hadn't heard correctly. "Uncle Eddie's got to give what—"

"No. That *is* the message. And I quote. 'He's got to give them back.'"

Kat shook her head. "I don't understand."

"There was a job, Kat. A week ago. In Italy."

"I haven't heard about any jobs," Kat insisted before remembering that she'd been out of the world. The loop. The life. She knew what the Colgan cafeteria was serving every day this month, but this…

"Private collection," Hale continued. "Very high-end paintings. Very high security. *Very high risk.* Two – maybe three – crews in the world could have done it, and—"

"My dad's at the top of the list?"

Hale shook his head. "There *is* no list. There's just—"

"Dad." Kat sat for a moment, thinking, then sighed. "So?" she asked. Suddenly it all seemed preposterous. "So what? This is what he does, Hale. This is what we all do. What makes this time any different?"

She stood and started for the door, but in a flash, Hale was standing; his hand was around her wrist.

"It's different because it's different, Kat. This guy – this guy with the paintings – he's a *bad* guy."

"I'm Bobby Bishop's daughter, Hale. I know a lot of bad guys."

She tried to pull away, but Hale's chest was pressed against hers. His hands were warm against her skin. There was a new urgency in his voice as he whispered, "Listen to me, Kat. He's not a bad guy like your dad and Uncle Eddie are bad guys." He took a deep breath. "Like *I'm* a bad guy. This guy? His name's Arturo Taccone, and he's a whole different kind of bad."

In the two years since she'd met him, Kat had seen Hale wear a lot of expressions: playful, intrigued, bored. But she had never seen him scared before, and that, more than anything, made her shiver.

"He wants his paintings back." Hale's voice was softer now. The hard edge had left him, and something else had settled in its place. "If he doesn't have them in two weeks, then…" Hale obviously didn't want to say what came next, which was just as well. Kat didn't want to hear it.

As she dropped back onto the sofa, Kat couldn't remember the last time she'd been speechless. Then again, she also couldn't remember the last time she'd been framed for a crime she didn't commit, kicked out of a boarding school that it had taken her three whole months to con her way into, and then, technically, kidnapped by a guy who could buy a Monet and yet couldn't resist stealing a Vermeer. Speechless seemed OK under the circumstances.

"My dad used to be more careful than this," she said softly.

"Your dad used to have you."

Kat ate her corned beef sandwich. She drank some lemonade. She was aware, faintly, of Hale watching her, but that was only because he was Hale, and the part of Kat that made her a girl wouldn't let her forget that he was in the room. Otherwise, she was as quiet as a church mouse. She would have made her family proud.

An hour later Marcus was leading Kat up the sweeping staircase, and Kat was staring, trying to guess whether the silver-haired man was closer in age to fifty or eighty. She was listening, trying to determine whether his accent was more Scottish than Welsh. But most of all, Kat was wondering why Marcus was the only servant she had ever seen orbiting around Planet Hale.

"I've taken the liberty of putting you in Mrs Hale's room, miss"

Marcus opened a wide set of double doors, and Kat started to protest – the mansion had fourteen bedrooms, after all. But then Marcus switched on the lights, and Kat breathed in the stale air of a room that was clean but neglected. It had a king-size bed, a chaise longue, and at least twenty silk-covered pillows, all in varying shades of blue. It was beautiful but sad, Kat thought. It needed to feel a beating heart.

"If there is anything you need, miss," Marcus told her from the door, "I'm number seven on the house phone."

"No," Kat mumbled. "I mean, yes. I mean…I don't need anything. Thank you."

"Very well, miss," he said, reaching for the doors.

"Marcus?" She stopped him. "Have Hale's parents…I mean Mr and Mrs Hale… How long will they be away?" Kat asked, wondering which was sadder: having parents who've died or ones who've simply floated away.

"The lady of the house will not be needing the room, miss"

"Are you ever going to call me Kat, Marcus?"

"Not today, miss" He repeated softly, "Not today."

He closed the door, and Kat listened to his footsteps receding down the long hallway. She lay down on Hale's mother's empty bed, the duvet cover cold against her skin. She felt very much alone in that big room, thinking about her dad and Uncle Eddie, about Porsche Speedsters and Monet.

Hours passed. Her thoughts blended together until they were like an Impressionist painting, and Kat knew she was too close to see anything plainly. She thought about crime, as she so often had in her fifteen years – ever since the day her father had told her he'd buy her ice cream if she would scream, and keep screaming until one of the guards outside the Tower of London left his post to see what was wrong.

She heard Hale's words: *He used to have you.*

Kat jumped from the bed and rifled through her bags until she found her passport. She flipped it open and saw the name Melanie O'Hara beside a picture of herself in a red wig. She dug again, flipped open another cover: Erica Sampson, a slender blonde. Three more tries yielded three more memories, until Kat found...herself.

She tucked those other girls away. For now. Then she picked up the phone and dialed. "Marcus?"

"Yes, miss," he replied, seeming too alert for four am.

"I think I may need to leave."

"Of course, miss If you'll look by the phone, you'll see I've already taken the liberty..."

Then Kat saw it – an envelope. A plane ticket. Eight am first class to Paris.

33

FOUR

Kat used to love Paris. She remembered being there with her parents – eating croissants, visiting a pyramid, and carrying six red balloons. It wasn't until years later that she realized it hadn't been a fun family outing – that actually they'd been casing the Louvre at the time. Still, the memories made her smile as she bought a pastry from her father's favourite café and carried it outside into the chilly wind. She shivered a little and wished she'd brought a warmer coat. Across the busy square, she saw the shop where her mother had bought her a pair of bright red patent leather shoes for Christmas. She wished a lot of things.

"I know Uncle Eddie says he's in Paris, but it might take a day or two to find him," she'd told Marcus as he dropped her off at the airport.

"Of course, miss," Marcus had said in a way that implied that he knew better; and somehow, as always, Marcus was right.

Bobby Bishop's name and address and phone number might be constantly changing, but Kat knew her father, and that, it turned out, was enough to track him down.

He was half a block away when she spotted him. The faintest hint of gray was settling into his dark hair, but it was still thick and slightly curly. He took long strides and kept the collar of his dark cashmere coat turned up against the wind as he walked – not too slow, not too fast – among the crowd.

Kat hurried back inside, bought a black coffee, and took the steaming cup outside, expecting to see him – to watch him stop in surprise at the sight of her. But when she returned to the street and scanned the crowd for his face and that familiar gait, he was gone. Had he passed her by? For a second she worried that she might not find him again. Or worse, that she might find him too late.

She set off in the direction he'd been going, and was about to call his name, when, on instinct, she stopped and turned around. There, in the centre of the square, she saw him standing amid a large group of tourists, listening to a guide who was lecturing at the fountain's edge.

Her father didn't seem to notice her weaving through the hordes of tourists and scavenging pigeons. There were no hugs or cries of hello when she stepped up beside him.

"I hope that's for me," her father said, but his gaze

never left the man who was speaking to the group in rapid Russian.

Kat didn't know whether to feel annoyed or impressed by his casual tone – as if this were a standing date, and he'd been expecting her all along.

She handed him his coffee, watched him wrap cold hands around the warm cup. "No gloves?" she asked.

He smiled and sipped. "Not on my day off."

Thieves aren't supposed to want too much – which is ironic, but true. Never live anywhere you can't walk away from. Never own anything you can't leave behind. These were the laws of Kat's life – of Kat's world. As she watched her father sip hot coffee and sneak smiles at her over the top of the cup, she knew that, strictly speaking, no thief is ever supposed to love anything as much as she loved him.

"Hi, Daddy."

Nearby, church bells started to ring. Pigeons scattered. And her father glanced at her from the corner of his eye and said, "I know the Colgan School is good, honey, but Paris seems an awfully long way to come for a field trip."

"Yeah, I know, but it's autumn break." Kat didn't want to know why lying to her father was far easier than telling her head-master the truth. "I wanted to see how you were doing."

Another sip. Another smile. But this time he didn't

meet her eyes. "You wanted to see if the rumours were true," he said, and Kat felt her face burn in the cold wind. "So, who told?" her father asked. "Uncle Eddie? Hale?" He shook his head and spoke through gritted teeth. "I'm gonna kill that kid."

"It wasn't his fault."

"Like Barcelona wasn't his fault?"

"Yeah, well..." Kat heard herself repeating Hale's words: "We all agreed that that monkey seemed perfectly well trained at the time."

Her father scoffed.

"Dad—"

"Sweetheart, would you believe me if I said I didn't pull any jobs in Italy last week?" The bells stopped, and the guide resumed his lecture. Kat's father glanced around the square and lowered his voice. "If I said I had an airtight alibi?"

"You have an alibi?" Kat asked. "You swear?"

Her father's eyes glowed. "On a Gutenberg Bible."

"You can prove it?"

"Well," he hesitated. "It's a little more complicated than..." But then he trailed off and the crowd shifted, revealing a newsstand – headlines calling out in black and white: *Nouveaux Pistes Dans le Vol de Galerie: La Police Dit Que les Arrestations Sont en Vue.*

"Dad," Kat said slowly, "you don't happen to know anything about that gallery that was robbed last week, do you?" His smile was part pride, part mischief, and yet he didn't face her. He didn't say a single word. "So you *didn't* do a big job in Italy last week because on the night in question you were doing a little job in Paris?"

He blew on the steaming coffee, then whispered, "I told you it was a good alibi." He took a small sip. "Of course the work wasn't quite up to my usual standards – you know my best assistant left me recently?" He shook his head and drew an exaggerated breath. "Good help is so hard to find."

One of the Russian ladies hissed, warning them to be quiet, and Kat started to feel claustrophobic. She wanted somewhere private. She wanted somewhere she could yell. Then suddenly Kat found herself wondering…

"Dad, if the job was last week, why are you still in Paris?"

As he paused mid-sip, Kat couldn't help but think that the thief had been caught, busted. The father, on the other hand, just seemed proud of his little girl.

"Sweetie, let's just say possession is nine tenths of the law, so right now I'm not as guilty as I might like to be."

"Dad…" She stared up at her father, not quite sure she wanted to know the answer to her next question: "Where'd you stash them?"

"*It*," he corrected, "is somewhere safe."

"Somewhere lonely?"

"No." Her father chuckled. "Unfortunately, at the moment, it has plenty of friends."

He continued to smile, but something about the way his eyes kept darting around the square made Kat worry.

"Then maybe you should leave it there," Kat suggested.

He rocked on his heels, but didn't meet her gaze. "Now what would be the fun in that?" He smiled wider, and Kat could have sworn she saw one of the Russian women swoon a little at the sight. A pair of teenage girls were whispering and giggling in their direction, but as far as Kat could tell, there was only one woman on the square who dared to openly stare. Perhaps she was too beautiful – too self-assured – to care who saw her looking. And yet this gorgeous, dark-haired woman's unwavering eyes made Kat feel strange.

"Watching women checking out my dad is creepy, you know?"

"Sweetheart" – her father's voice was steady – "sometimes it can't be helped."

He was teasing, Kat thought. Wasn't he? But as they started to follow the tour group to the steps of a nearby church, Kat still felt the staring, as if someone were watching her every move.

Kat pulled a tiny camera from her purse and scanned the crowd. A man sat beneath an umbrella at a pavement café, not eating. She zoomed in on two men who lingered on a bench at the corner of the square, and recognized the plain clothes, bad shoes, and haggard look of a surveillance team five days into a job. And finally, Kat studied the woman standing at the edge of the square, staring at her father, who had barely met Kat's eyes since she'd found him.

"So who are your friends?" She turned back and sighed. "Local cops?"

"Interpol, actually."

"*Nice*," Kat said, drawing out the word.

"I thought you'd be impressed."

"It's every little girl's dream," she said. "Interpol surveillance. And kittens."

The church bells started to chime again. A bus pulled to a stop in front of them, blocking their view of the square, sheltering them from prying eyes, and in that split second, Kat's father reached for her, gripping her shoulders. "Look, Kat. I don't want you to worry about this thing – this Italy thing. No one's going to hurt me. This guy doesn't care about me. He cares about his paintings, and I don't have them, so…" He shrugged.

"He *thinks* you have them."

"But I *don't*," he said in that no-nonsense kind of way that all good fathers and great thieves are born with. "I've got a twenty-four-hour tail and a solid alibi. Trust me, Kat. *Taccone isn't going to come for me.*"

She almost believed him. She wondered if he believed it himself. But Kat had learned at a very young age that thieves live and die based on perception – her whole life was a lesson in sleight of hand. If someone *thought* her father had the paintings, then the truth wasn't going to save him.

"You've got to talk to him," Kat pleaded. "Or hide, or run, or—"

"Give it till the end of the week, Kat. He'll turn over enough rocks, and enough things will crawl out that he'll figure out the truth."

"Dad—" she started, but it was too late. The bus was moving and her father was already pulling away, his lips barely moving as he said, "So where does your school think you are right now? Do you need me to write you a note?"

"You already did," Kat lied. "It was faxed directly to Headmaster Franklin from your London office yesterday morning."

"That's my girl," he whispered, and the previous unpleasant conversation seemed a million years ago. "Now go on, get back to school."

Kat stalled, not knowing whether she should admit to him that she'd been kicked out – that the biggest job she'd ever pulled had just blown up in her face – or whether to let the con live on.

"Do they give you a winter break at the Colgan School?" His gaze was locked on the guide at the front of the group. "I was thinking about Cannes for Christmas."

"Cannes for Christmas," Kat echoed softly.

"Or maybe Madrid?" he asked.

Kat held back a grin and whispered, "Surprise me."

"Kat." His voice stopped her. She even risked looking at him, framed by the ancient church and cobblestone square. "I don't suppose you can help your old man out?"

Kat smiled and started through the crowd, clutching her camera, just another tourist. When she saw a pair of Paris cops and shouted, "Excuse me!" she sounded like an ordinary girl on the verge of panic. She had a death grip on her purse and looked utterly helpless as she rushed towards them. "Excuse me, officer!"

"Yes?" one of the cops said in accented English. "Is something wrong?"

"Those men!" Kat screamed, pointing at the two plainclothes Interpol officers who had left the café and were now chatting with their colleague on the bench.

"They tried to get me to…" Kat trailed off. The cops looked impatient but intrigued.

"Yes?"

"They…" Kat gestured for one of the cops to come closer, then whispered in his ear. In a flash, both men were pushing through the crowd.

"Vous là!" the cop called to the surveillance team in rapid French. *"Vous là! Arrêtez!"* The Interpol officers were almost to the fountain when the cops called again. *"J'ai dit arrêtez!"*

The men tried to pull away, but it was too late. People were staring. The cops were bearing down. French obscenities were flying. Pockets were searched and ID.s were studied, and through it all, the pigeons kept scavenging, the bells kept ringing.

And Kat knew that her father was already gone.

She turned her back on the chaos, ready for a taxi and a long, quiet plane ride over the Atlantic. But suddenly, someone grasped her arms. She heard a car door open behind her, and for the second time in two days, she found herself in the back of a limo, greeted by another unexpected voice.

"Hello, Katarina."

FIVE

The only person who consistently called Kat by her full name was Uncle Eddie, but the man in the back of the car could not have been more different from her great-uncle. She studied him – his cashmere coat and matching suit, his silk tie and slicked-back hair, and she remembered Hale's warning: *He's a different kind of bad.* Her first thought was to fight, but two men were settling into place on either side of her, and Kat knew it wasn't an option. So instead she asked, "I don't suppose you'll let me go if I ask nicely?"

The man's thin lips broke into a smile. "I was told you had your father's sense of humour." His dark eyes remained cold as he studied her. "And that you have your mother's eyes."

Despite the circumstances, that was what caught Kat off guard. "You knew my mother?"

"I knew *of* her," he corrected. "She was a very talented

woman. I'm told she too was like a cat. That is what you prefer to be called, is it not, Katarina?"

His English bore a faint accent she couldn't place – not entirely Italian – as if he were a citizen of the world.

"You have very good sources," she said.

"I have the best of everything." The man smiled. "My name is Arturo Taccone."

"What do you want?"

"I thought I might give you a ride to the airport." He gestured around the interior of the beautiful antique car, but Kat merely shrugged.

"I'd planned on taking a cab."

He laughed. "But that would be such a waste. Besides, this way, you and I can have a nice talk. And along the way we can even pick up my paintings if you'd prefer."

"I don't have them," she blurted before realizing how the words might sound. "My *father* doesn't have them either." She leaned toward him, hoping that proximity might equal believability. "Look, he didn't do it. You're staking out the wrong guy. He was doing a gallery job in Paris that night. Stop. Get a paper. It's on the front—"

"Katarina," Taccone interrupted, his whisper more terrifying than a shout. "These paintings are very important to me. I came to Paris to explain that to your father, but at the moment he is a bit too popular for my taste." Kat thought about the Interpol officers watching her father's every move. "So it is most fortunate that I should meet *you*. I want my paintings back, Katarina. I am willing to go to a great deal of trouble – to take a great many *pains*, if you will – to get them back. You will tell your father this for me?"

As Kat sat across from Arturo Taccone, sandwiched between the two massive men who never left his shadow, she had yet to hear the stories. She was ignorant of his dealings in the Middle East. She hadn't heard about the explosions at his warehouse near Berlin or the mysterious disappearance of a bank manager in Zurich. She knew only what she saw: a well-dressed man, an antique walking stick with an ornately carved pewter handle, two guards, and absolutely no way out.

"He can't return what he didn't steal," Kat pleaded, but the elegant man only laughed a slow cold laugh and called to the driver.

"Two weeks should be enough time, don't you think? Of course, it should take less, but out of respect for your mother and her family, I'll be generous."

The limo slowed to a stop. The goons opened the doors, and as Arturo Taccone stepped out into the sunshine of the Paris street, he said, "It was a pleasure meeting you, Katarina." He laid a business card on the seat beside her. "Until we meet again."

It wasn't until the door slammed and the car started through the busy streets toward the airport, that Kat felt herself begin to breathe in slow ragged breaths. She stared down at the white card that bore Arturo Taccone's name printed in plain black letters. And the handwritten words: *Two weeks.*

"He didn't do it."

Kat spoke from the doorway of a dark room, towards the silhouetted figure in the massive bed. She saw it jump upright, felt the lights flash on, stinging her eyes. But she was far too tired to blink against the glare.

"Kat," Hale groaned, then fell back onto the pillows. "Funny, I didn't hear a doorbell."

"I let myself in; hope that's OK."

Hale smiled. "Or the alarm."

She stepped inside, tossed a pocket-size bag of tools onto the bed. "You're due for an upgrade."

Hale propped himself up against the antique headboard and squinted up at her. "She returns." He crossed his arms across his bare chest. "You know, I could be naked in here."

But Kat didn't allow herself to think about what Hale was or was not wearing underneath those Egyptian cotton sheets. "He didn't do it, Hale." She dropped into a chair by the fireplace. "My dad has an alibi."

"You believe him?"

"Normally?" Kat asked. "Maybe." Then she shrugged and admitted, "Maybe not." She looked down at her hands. "But I'm pretty sure he couldn't have been pulling a big job in Italy on the same night he was pulling a small job in Paris."

Hale let out a slow whistle of admiration, and Kat remembered that, for all of his resources and talent, the most dangerous thing about W. W. Hale the Fifth was that, when he grew up, he really wanted to be her father.

"He's still in Paris?" Hale asked. Kat nodded. He swung his bare feet to the floor and looked at her. "So...what? He's got the loot stashed somewhere and a twenty-four-hour tail keeping him from recovering it and leaving town?"

"Something like that."

"What's he gonna do?"

"Nothing."

Hale shook his head. "You Bishops...one of you won't leave" – he cut his eyes at her – "and one of you won't stop running away."

Without even realizing she'd done it, Kat pulled a card from her pocket and ran a finger across the heavy paper. "What's that?" Hale asked.

Kat looked toward the dying fire and felt herself tremble. "Arturo Taccone's business card."

In a flash, Hale had thrown the covers aside and moved towards her. Part of Kat couldn't help but notice that no, he wasn't naked, but other parts – the thief part and the daughter part and the part that had seen the darkness in Taccone's eyes – barely noticed the Superman pyjama bottoms. "Please tell me you found that on a pavement somewhere," Hale said.

"He was probably there following Dad, but then he saw me and...he gave me a ride to the airport."

"Arturo Taccone gave you a ride to the airport?"

Hale's hair was sticking up at strange angles, but even as Kat said, "Nice pants," she knew there was nothing funny about the situation.

"Kat, tell me you weren't alone with Arturo Taccone."

"I'm fine."

"You're fine?" Hale snapped. "I'm telling you, Kat. Uncle Eddie says this guy means business, and Uncle Eddie—"

"Ought to know. I know."

"This isn't a game, Kat."

"Do I look like I'm playing, Hale?"

Hale kicked at the fallen covers, and to Kat he looked like a man who was scared and a little boy who hadn't got his way. Both. After a long silence, he said, "Well, did you at least tell him he's after the wrong guy?"

"Of course I did, but he wasn't exactly in the mood to take my word for it."

"Kat, you've got to—"

"What?" Kat cut in. "Hale, what am I supposed to do? My dad doesn't have the paintings. There's no way this Taccone guy is ever going to believe he doesn't have the paintings, so what? Should I tell my father to go into hiding so he'll have a nice head start when the biggest goons money can buy start chasing him in two weeks? I don't know about you, but the fact that he's got an Interpol surveillance detail watching him twenty-four-seven feels pretty good to me right now!"

"This guy really wants his paintings back."

"So we're going to *give* him his paintings back."

"Great plan. Except we don't have the paintings."

"We will," Kat said as she stood and started for the door. "Just as soon as we steal them."

13 DAYS
UNTIL DEADLINE

NEW YORK,
USA

SIX

An odd thing tends to happen on the cusp of winter. Ask any better-than-average thief and he'll tell you that the best time to pull a con is when the weather should be changing – but isn't. People feel lucky. Marks get careless. They look at the sky and know the snow is up there somewhere, and so they think about how they've already cheated Mother Nature. Perhaps they could get away with much, much more.

If Kat had any doubt about this theory, all she had to do was glance around Madison Square Park as she and Hale strolled down Fifth Avenue. The sun was warm but the wind was cool, and children played without their hats and scarves. Nannies chatted beside expensive pushchair, while businesspeople took the long way home. And that was when she saw him.

Kat would not have described him as handsome. She'd been raised by Bobby Bishop, after all, and had spent entirely too much time around Hale. *Handsome* isn't a synonym for attractive; and while the man walking through the square wasn't the former, he certainly was the latter.

His hair, for example, was slick and gelled. His suit was the kind of expensive that would be out of style far too soon, and his watch was the only thing about him that was as shiny as his teeth. And yet, for the purposes of Kat's world, he was – put simply – perfect.

"Oh boy," Kat heard herself mutter as the man traipsed forward, his gaze glued to his mobile, and ran right into a bumbling old man in a long trench coat and mismatched socks.

"Oh boy," Hale echoed.

"Are you OK?" Kat overheard the slick man ask. The old man nodded but gripped the lapels of the other man's expensive suit, steadying himself.

As the two men parted ways, one stopped after only a single step. But the perfect man – the perfect mark – kept walking. He was well out of earshot by the time Kat waved at the rumpled vagrant and said, "Hello, Uncle Eddie."

If Kat had stayed at Colgan long enough, a teacher might have eventually told her what her family had been saying for generations: It's OK to break the rules, but only sometimes, and only if you know them very, very well.

So maybe that was why, among the world's great thieves, Uncle Eddie and Uncle Eddie alone was allowed the luxury of a permanent address.

Stepping inside the old Brooklyn brownstone, Kat felt the sun disappear behind a heavy wooden door, blocking out a neighbourhood that had spent the last sixty years morphing from trendy to shady and back again. But inside, nothing ever changed. The hallway was always dim. The air always smelled like the Old Country, or what she'd been told the Old Country smelled like: cabbage and carrots and things simmering for long hours over slow heat in cast-iron pots that would outlive them all.

It was, in a word, home, and yet Kat didn't dare say so.

Uncle Eddie shuffled down the narrow hallway, stopping only long enough to pull the slick man's wallet from his pocket and toss it onto a pile of nearly identical loot that sat unopened. Forgotten.

"You've been keeping busy." Kat chose one of the wallets and thumbed through the contents: one I.D., four credit cards, and nine hundred dollars in cash that hadn't been touched. "Uncle Eddie, there's a lot of money in—"

"Take off your shoes if you're coming in," her great-uncle barked as he continued down the narrow hall. Hale kicked off his Italian loafers, but Kat was already hurrying behind her uncle, trailing him into the heart of the house.

"You're picking pockets?" Kat asked once they reached the kitchen.

Her uncle stood quietly at the ancient stove that dominated the far wall.

"Tell me you're being careful," Kat went on. "It's not like the old days, Uncle Eddie. Now every street corner has an ATM, and every ATM has a camera, and—"

But she might as well have been speaking to a deaf man. Uncle Eddie pulled two porcelain bowls from the shelf above the stove and began ladling soup. He handed one bowl to Hale and one to Kat and pointed them towards a long wooden table surrounded by mismatched chairs. Hale sat and ate as if he hadn't had a decent meal in weeks, but Kat stayed standing.

"It's a different world, Uncle Eddie. I just don't want you to get into trouble."

Just then, Hale's spoon scraped the bottom of his bowl. There was no hiding the dismay in his voice as he asked, "UncleEddie, why is the seal of the British Royal Family on your dishes?"

Her uncle's voice was gruff, impatient. "Because that's who I was with when I stole them."

As Kat held the bowl in her hands, she couldn't help but realize it was hot – in a lot of ways. She couldn't help but see Uncle Eddie as Hale saw him – not as an old man, but as *the* old man.

"We practise a very old art, Katarina." Her uncle paused long enough to toss Hale's wallet towards him. "It is kept alive not by blood" – another pause as Uncle Eddie dropped Kat's passport onto the counter next to a loaf of day-old bread – "but by practice."

The old man turned away from his speechless niece and the boy she had brought home. "I suppose you were absent the day they taught that at the Colgan School."

Kat's coat suddenly felt too heavy as she stood there, remembering that she couldn't take the heat and *that* was why she'd got out of the kitchen. She sat down at the table, knowing that now she was back in.

There were a lot of things that could have happened next. Uncle Eddie might have commented that the boy Kat had brought home dressed far better than the stray her mother had chosen. Hale might have worked up the courage to finally ask Uncle Eddie the story behind the fake Rembrandt that hung above the hearth. Kat might have admitted that the food services department at Colgan had nothing on her uncle's cooking. But when the back door slammed open, everyone's attention was on the two boys who hurried in, struggling to restrain the largest, shaggiest dog that Kat had ever seen.

"Uncle Eddie, we're back!" The smaller boy tightened his grip on the dog's collar. "They were out of Dalmatians, but we got a…" He looked up. "Hey, Kat's here! With Hale!" Hamish Bagshaw was slightly shorter and stockier than his older brother, but otherwise, the ruddy English boys could have passed for twins. The dog lurched, and Hamish hardly noticed. "Hey, Kat, I thought you were at…"

When he trailed off, Kat told herself it was the heat from the stove that was making her face red. She focused on breathing in the fresh air from the open door, and swore she didn't care what anyone thought. Still, she was relieved to hear Hale ask, "So, Angus, how's the bum?"

Her relief quickly faded when Angus started unbuttoning his trousers. "Good as new. German docs fixed me right up. You wanna see the scar?"

"No!" Kat said, but what she thought was: They were in Germany?

They did a job in Germany.

They did a job without me.

She looked at Hale, watched the way he licked his spoon and helped himself to a second bowl of soup, at home in her uncle's kitchen. She looked at her uncle, who hadn't even smiled at her. And when she turned to the Bagshaw boys, Kat couldn't meet their gaze. Instead she focused on the mangy mutt between them and whispered, "Dog in a bar."

"Hey, you guys want in?" Angus asked, beaming.

"Boys," Uncle Eddie warned, as if saving Kat from the shame of admitting that even classic cons were beyond her now.

"Sorry, Uncle Eddie," the brothers mumbled in unison. They eased quietly out of the kitchen, taking the mutt back into the night without another word. Then Uncle Eddie took his place at the head of the table.

"You have to ask the question, Katarina, in order for this old man to answer."

The last time Kat had been in this room, it had been August. The air outside had felt like the air in the kitchen was then – sticky and thick. At the time, Kat had thought she would never again be so uncomfortable at her uncle's table. Sure, this was where her father had planned the De Beers diamond heist when she was three. It was the very room where her uncle had orchestrated the hijacking of eighty percent of the world's caviar when she was seven. But nothing had ever felt as criminal as sitting there, announcing to her uncle that her greatest con had worked and she was walking away from her family's kitchen in order to steal an education from one of the best schools in the world.

Turns out, that was nothing compared to walking back in and saying, "Uncle Eddie, we need your help." She lowered her eyes, studied a century's worth of scuffs and scars in the wood beneath her hands. "*I* need your help."

Uncle Eddie walked over to the oven and pulled out a loaf of fresh bread. Kat closed her eyes and thought of warm croissants and cobblestone streets. "He didn't do it, Uncle Eddie. I flew to Paris and talked to Dad. He has an alibi, but..."

"Arturo Taccone paid Kat a visit," Hale finished for her.

Kat could count on one hand the number of times she'd seen her great-uncle genuinely surprised; this was *not* one of them. She knew it the moment he turned from the stove and looked at Hale with knowing eyes. "Your job was to deliver a message."

"Yes, sir," Hale told him. "I did that."

"Nineteen fifty-eight was a good year for cars, young man."

"Yes, sir."

"Arturo Taccone is not the sort of man I would like visiting my great-niece."

"She left in the middle of the night. She does that." Hale glanced away then added a quick, "Sir."

It felt, in that moment, as if her going to school was all the excuse anyone had ever needed to start treating Kat like a child. "*She* is sitting right here!" Kat didn't realize she was yelling until her uncle looked at her in the manner of a man who has not been yelled at in a very long time.

"I'm *here*," Kat said in a softer voice.

She didn't say, *I can hear you.*

She didn't tell him, *I came home.*

She didn't promise, *I'm not going anywhere.*

There were at least a dozen things that she might have said to reclaim her place at the table, but there was only one that really mattered. "Taccone wants his paintings back."

Uncle Eddie studied her. "Of course he does."

"But Dad doesn't have them."

"Your father isn't one to ask for help, Katarina, especially not from me."

"Uncle Eddie, *I* need your help."

She watched her uncle take a long serrated knife from a block by the stove and slice three pieces of warm bread. "What can I do?" Uncle Eddie asked in his *I'm just an old man* tone.

"I need to know who did the Taccone job," Kat told him.

He rolled back to the table, handed her a piece of bread and a plate of butter. "And why would you need to know that?" he asked. But it wasn't a question – it was a test. Of knowledge. Of loyalty. Of how far Kat was willing to crawl to get back to where she'd been last summer.

"Because whoever did the Taccone job has Taccone's paintings."

"*And…*"

Kat and Hale looked at each other. "And we're going to steal them." Kat felt a surge of strength as she said the words. Like confession, it was good for the soul.

"Eat your bread, Katarina," Uncle Eddie told her, and Kat obeyed. It was the first meal she'd had since Paris.

"This is a serious thing you're trying to do," Uncle Eddie said. "Who, may I ask, is this *we* of which you speak?"

Hale looked at her. He opened his mouth to answer, but Kat cut him off. "Hale and I can do it."

"Then this is a *very* serious thing. I'm afraid it might be difficult to accomplish from the Colgan School…"

If the stories were to be believed, Uncle Eddie had once won a million dollars in one weekend playing cards in Monte Carlo. Without cheating. For the first time in her life, Kat believed in the power of her uncle's poker face.

She lowered her gaze and told her uncle what he already knew: "It turns out the Colgan School and I have had a parting of ways."

"I see." Her uncle nodded but didn't gloat. He didn't have to.

"We need a name, Uncle Eddie," Hale said.

"People genuinely like your father, Katarina." Uncle Eddie thumbed his nose and muttered, "Although *why*, I do not understand. But he has friends." He placed a rough hand on top of hers. "Let me make some calls. It might take a day or—"

"We don't have a day or two." Kat felt herself growing angry. "We know you can find out who did the Taccone job, Uncle Eddie." She stood up, towering over her uncle for the first – and probably last – time in her life. "If you can't or won't tell us, we'll find someone who will. But it has to be done." She drew a deep breath. "*I* have to do it."

"Finish your soup, Katarina," Uncle Eddie said, but Kat didn't sit; she didn't eat. She watched her uncle stand and walk to the pantry; but instead of some rich dessert, he pulled out a thick roll of long paper.

Hale glanced at her, his eyes wide as her uncle pushed their meals away and laid the roll on the end of the table.

"The man who did the Taccone job..." Uncle Eddie began slowly. Maybe it was fatigue or habit, but his accent seemed thicker than normal as he leaned over the scroll. "We don't know *who* he is. We don't know *where* he is." Kat's heart beat faster while her spirits fell. Then, Uncle Eddie gave a flick of his wrist and, in a flash, the scroll unfurled on the long table, and Kat's eyes settled on the most elaborate blueprints she'd ever seen.

Her uncle smiled. "But we know *where he's been*."

The street was dark by the time they left the brownstone. Maybe Kat had been too long in the hot kitchen, but without the sun, the air really did feel like winter, as if they'd been inside long enough for the season to finally change.

Hale walked beside her, buttoning his heavy wool coat. Kat shivered, and when he put his arm around her, she didn't push him away. They blended into the scenery – two kids out for a walk to the library. Maybe a movie or a slice of pizza. Just a boy and a girl. Just a couple.

Heavy drops of drizzle landed on Hale's dark coat and shone like beads of silver.

"You ever seen that much security on one set of blueprints before?" he asked.

Kat shook her head. "No."

"So whoever did it was really smart," Hale said.

Kat thought about the cool indifference with which Arturo Taccone had threatened her father's life, and added, "And really stupid."

Hale was silhouetted against the streetlamp's yellow light, but the glint in his eyes was unmistakable. "Remind you of anyone we know?"

12 DAYS
UNTIL DEADLINE

LAS VEGAS,
USA

SEVEN

There are a lot of reasons people come to Las Vegas. Some come because they want to get rich. Some come because they want to get married. Some want to get lost, and others found. Some are running to. Some are running from. It had always seemed to Kat that Vegas was a town where almost everyone was hoping to get something for nothing – an entire city of thieves.

But as Kat and Hale rode the escalator from the casino floor to the conference rooms above, she realized those reasons probably did not apply to the International Association of Advanced Mathematics and Research.

"I didn't know there were this many maths guys," Hale said as they stepped onto the crowded concourse. Kat cleared her throat. "And women," he added. "Maths women."

Everywhere Kat looked, she saw men wearing bad suits and name badges, mingling and laughing, oblivious to the slot machines and cocktail waitresses only a floor below. Kat supposed the keynote speaker must be as brilliant and riveting as the rumours said. *If you were interested in derivatives, theorems, and polynomials, that is.* Kat and Hale followed the crowd into the dim ballroom where the man was lecturing. They found seats in the back row.

"So these are the smartest people in the world, huh?" Hale whispered.

Kat scanned the crowd. "At least one of them is."

Hale's gaze was locked on the conference programme he held in his hands. "Where is he?"

"By the projector. Fifth row. Centre aisle."

At the front of the room, the professor rambled on in a language that only a few people in the world could truly understand.

"You know" – Hale's breath was warm against Kat's ear in the chilly ballroom – "I don't know that both of us really have to be here…" The slide changed. While hundreds of mathematicians waited with bated breath, the boy beside Kat whispered, "I could go make some calls…check on some things…"

"Play some blackjack?"

"Well, when in Rome…"

"Rome is tomorrow, babe," Kat reminded him.

He nodded. "Right."

"Shh."

"Do you understand any of this?" he said, pointing to the lines and symbols that covered the massive screens.

"Some people understand the value of an education."

Hale stretched and crossed his legs, then settled his arm around Kat's shoulders. "That's sweet, Kat. Maybe later I'll buy you a university. And an ice cream."

"I'd settle for the ice cream."

"Deal."

They stayed in the overly air-conditioned ballroom, listening to the entire first lecture and part of the second. By the time she saw a member of the hotel's audiovisual staff slink out the back doors, Kat's hands were frozen and her stomach was growling. So she didn't think twice about grabbing Hale and slipping through the open door.

While the maths genius droned on inside Ballroom B, three teenagers gathered secretly in the empty casino hallway.

No one overheard Hale say, "Hi, Simon."

"So you tell us, how was the lecture, Simon?" Hale paused and read the name tag of the boy in front of him. "Or is it Henry?"

But the boy just smiled as if he'd been caught – which

he had – by two of the few people on earth whose opinions actually mattered to him.

"How'd you find me?" Simon asked. Hale just raised his eyebrows, and Simon muttered, "Never mind."

Soon the escalator was taking them away from the PhDs and carpeted ballrooms; the silence gave way to ringing machines and screaming tourists. Kat practically had to yell as she asked, "How's your dad?"

"Retired," Simon answered. "Again. Florida this time, I think."

"Retired?" Hale didn't try to hide his shock. "He's *forty-three*."

"People do crazy things when they hit the prime numbers," Simon explained with a shrug. He leaned closer. "He's actually been consulting with Seabold Security."

"Judas," Hale teased.

But Kat barely heard. She was too busy scanning the casino. Tourists in bumbags sat in rows at slot machines. Waitresses glided through the crowd. It was easy to feel alone there, lost in the chaos. But Kat was a thief. Kat knew better.

She patted the cylindrical case in her hands and looked at the boys beside her. "Let's go find a blind spot."

As they walked through the maze of the casino floor, Kat couldn't help but notice a slight bounce in Simon's step as he chatted on about the lecture, the advances in technology. The geniuses and legends who'd given talks that morning at breakfast.

"You know you're smarter than all of them, right?" Hale said flatly. "In fact, if you wanted to *prove* it..." He glanced at the blackjack tables.

Simon shook his head. "I don't count cards, Hale."

"Don't?" Hale smiled. "Or won't? You know, technically, it's not illegal."

"But it's frowned upon." Sweat beaded at Simon's brow. He sounded like someone had just suggested he swim after eating...run with scissors... "It is *seriously* frowned upon."

They found a table outside, near the edge of the crowded pool, away from cameras and guards.

Simon dragged his chair beneath an umbrella. "I burn," he explained as Kat took the seat across from him. He took a deep breath, as if working up the courage to ask, "Is it a job?"

Hale stretched out on a lounge chair, his eyes hidden behind dark sunglasses. "More like a favour."

Simon seemed to deflate, so Kat added, "For now."

The desert air was dry, but there was no denying the smell of chlorine – and money – as Kat rolled the blueprints out onto the glass tabletop.

Simon leaned over the plans. "Are these the Macaraff 760s?"

"Yep," Hale answered.

He whistled in the same way Hale sometimes whistled, but Simon's sounded more like a wounded bird.

"That's a lot of security. Bank?" he guessed. Kat shook her head. "Government?" Simon guessed again.

"Art," Kat said.

"Private collection," Hale added.

Simon glanced up from the table. "Yours?"

Hale laughed. "I wish."

"Is it our objective to make it yours?" Simon's eyes grew wide.

Hale and Kat exchanged a look. Hale's grin seemed to admit that the thought had crossed his mind. Then he leaned closer and said, "It's not exactly a typical operation."

Simon wasn't fazed; his mind was too full of theories and algorithms and exponential alternatives for *typical* to have any meaning for him anymore.

He studied the blueprints in silence for ten minutes, before looking up at Kat. "In my professional opinion, I'd say it's a pass. Unless this place is Fort Knox. Wait a second." His eyes shone. "*Is* it Fort Knox?"

"No," Hale and Kat said in unison.

"Then I wouldn't hit it," he said, pushing the blueprints away.

"It's already been hit," Kat confided.

"Your dad?"

"Why does everyone keep saying that?" Kat exclaimed.

Hale took off his sunglasses to look Simon in the eyes. His voice barely carried over the sounds of the laughter and splashes from the pool. "We would like very much to know who hit it."

"Who hit *this*?" Simon jabbed his finger at the centre of the blueprints. "It's not a big list, I can tell you that."

"The smaller the better, my friend," Hale said with a pat on Simon's back. "The smaller the better."

"Can I keep these?" Simon asked.

"Sure," Kat said. "We've got a spare set. And, Simon... thanks."

She was already standing and starting to walk away, when Simon asked, "This is why you're back, isn't it?"

Kat squinted against the bright sun. She felt a million miles from the grey-skied campus of Colgan.

"Yeah." She glanced at Hale. "It's kind of..."

Simon waved her away. "I don't need to know. I was just wondering if it had anything to do with those two guys who have been following us since we left the lecture."

* * *

Of all the people Kat expected to see on the Las Vegas strip, Arturo Taccone's goons were not on the list. They hadn't tried to blend in among the tourists and high rollers – hadn't taken a place at the tables, or positioned themselves by the slots – and that, more than anything, infuriated her. Together, Goon 1 and Goon 2 were five hundred pounds of European muscle.

And yet Kat had missed them.

She worried what else she might be missing as she rushed Hale and Simon away from the pool.

When Kat looked back, she saw Goon 2 raising his left arm, pointing at his watch.

"Kat?" Simon asked.

"Keep walking."

"What time is it?" Kat wondered aloud as she and Hale walked across the tarmac to the Hale family's private plane. "Let me think… Twelve hours in the air… That'll put us there—"

"High noon," Hale answered. "Give or take."

"OK, first thing tomorrow we hit the streets around Taccone's place. Somebody saw something."

"I got it covered."

"The DiMarcos might be in town."

"Actually, they're in jail."

"All seven of them?"

Hale shrugged. "It was an interesting October."

Kat shook her head and tried to tell herself that not everything had changed. "OK, then we should call—"

"I said, I've got it." Hale's voice was firmer now. Kat stopped in her tracks and stared at him.

"Define *got it*."

"Hey, I'm more than just a delightful travel companion, you know." He grinned. "I'm not exactly friendless."

"Who?" Kat asked.

But Hale kept walking. "A *friend*."

Kat reached for his arm and stopped him. "A friend of yours? A friend of mine? Or a friend of ours?"

He broke free of her grip and stepped away, hands in his pockets and a dark smile on his face. "Are we going to have a problem, Katarina?" he asked, sounding eerily like Uncle Eddie.

"What?" she asked, feigning innocence. "I'm just wondering who he is? Someone you and the Bagshaws used in Germany?"

"Luxembourg, actually." Hale paused and turned around. "Technically, the Bagshaws and I did a job in Luxembourg." Kat started to say something – wanted to say something – but the words didn't come. "You were gone, Kat." Hale wasn't teasing anymore.

"I know."

"You were at Colgan."

"I was only there three months."

"That's a long time, Kat. In our world, that's a long time." He took a deep breath. "Besides, your heart left a long time before the rest of you followed."

"Well, I'm back now." She started for the plane. "And there's a really small list of people who can do this thing, and an even smaller list you can trust to do it, so—"

"Your dad and Uncle Eddie weren't the only people you left when you went away, you know." Kat heard the words fly towards her across the tarmac. She turned, remembering the stale air of Hale's mother's room, and she knew she was looking at the one person in her life who was more used to being left than leaving.

He looked away, then back again. "Either we're a team or we aren't. Either you trust me or you don't." Hale took a step towards her. "What's it going to be, Kat?"

It is an occupational hazard that anyone who has spent her life learning how to lie eventually becomes bad at telling the truth; in that moment, Kat didn't have a clue what to say. *I can't do this without you* sounded trite. What they were doing was too big for a simple *Please*.

"Hale, I—"

"You know what? Never mind. Either way, I'm in, Kat."

He seemed utterly resolved as he slipped on his sunglasses. "I'm all in."

She watched him climb the stairs to the plane, heard him call over his shoulder, "Besides, I do make excellent arm candy."

Kat wanted to agree. She tried to say thank you. But all she managed to do was worry about who – or what – might be waiting on the ground in Italy.

11 DAYS
UNTIL DEADLINE

SABINA VALLEY,
ITALY

EIGHT

No *way*. Kat heard the words in her head before she thought to say them aloud. *No, Hale. No. Just…no.* Kat shook the sleep out of her head and tried to think clearly about the situation. After all, she was in Italy. With a smart and handsome boy. Standing on a private jet. The world lay quite literally at her feet, and yet, all Katarina Bishop could do was watch the door ease open, revealing a private airstrip, one of the most beautiful valleys in the world, and a young woman with long flowing hair and a cocked hip.

All she could say was, "No way."

It is fairly safe to assume that all thieves (or anyone who has spent much of their life in the dark) will have a sixth sense that allows them to hear more, process more quickly. And yet Kat wondered why the sight of that particular girl made the little hairs on her neck stand on end.

"Hello, Kitty Kat."

Oh yeah. That was it.

"Can I talk to you?" Kat grabbed at Hale, but even though she was very catlike on her feet, Hale was much sturdier on his. He moved past her and down the stairs just as the girl levelled her gaze at him and said, "Hey, handsome."

When he hugged the girl, her long legs left the ground, and Kat wanted to point out that it was far too cold for such a short skirt. She longed to note that high heels were a very bad idea in a city full of cobblestones. But Kat just stood frozen at the top of the stairs, not moving until the girl said, "Oh, come on, Kitty, don't you have a hug for your cousin?"

Families are strange things – living things – in more ways than one. And family businesses...well, there was no limit to the oddness.

Walking through the narrow streets of the small town Arturo Taccone called home, Kat had to wonder for the millionth time if it was that way in *all* family businesses. Was there a shoe shop in Seattle that had been handed down through generations only to spawn two teenage girls who couldn't be left alone together? Was there – at this very moment – a restaurant in Rio where two cousins were crossing their arms and refusing to work the same shift?

Or perhaps these feelings were reserved for the family businesses where people are occasionally shot. Or imprisoned. But Kat would never know. She only had one family, after all, and nothing whatsoever to compare it to.

"Hale," Gabrielle whined as she draped her arm through his, "Kat's not being very nice to me."

"Kat," Hale said as if enjoying playing grown-up, "hug your cousin."

But Kat never forced affection. And unlike Gabrielle, she adamantly refused to whine. Maybe she'd lost those abilities when she lost her mother; or maybe, like bad reflexes and a steadfast relationship with the truth, those skills were slowly being bred out of her family. Whatever the case, she managed to say, "It's good to see you, Gabrielle. I thought you were in Monte Carlo. The Eurotrash circuit."

"And I thought you were in study hall. Guess we were both mistaken."

Kat studied her cousin and wondered how it was possible that she was only a year older – not even that. Nine months. And yet she looked nine years more mature. She was taller, curvier, and just in general *more*. As she pressed against Hale, she held his arm tightly, leaving Kat to walk beside them like a third wheel down streets that were barely wide enough for two.

"So, where's Alfred?" Gabrielle asked.

"You mean Marcus?" Hale corrected.

"Whatever." The girl dismissed her mistake with a wave, and Kat thought it was too bad that her head hadn't filled out quite as completely as her bra. But then her cousin said, "Happy birthday," and a package of photos suddenly vanished from her hand and appeared in Hale's jacket pocket.

The pass was smooth. Effortless. The practised move of a seasoned pro, a member of the family.

"How's your mom?" Kat asked her.

"Engaged." Gabrielle gave an exasperated sigh. "Again."

"Oh," Hale said. "Congratulations."

"You could say that. He's a count. I think. Or maybe a duke." She turned to Hale. "Which one's better?"

Before he could answer, they came to a low stone wall. Beyond it, vineyards stretched out across the Sabina Valley. A river sliced through the fertile land while sheep grazed on a distant hill. Italy was one of the most beautiful places on earth, and yet Kat was unable to tear her eyes away from the photos in Hale's hands. Images of a massive compound near a beautiful lake. Hale leaned against the wall, flipping through the photos that zoomed in closer and closer to the compound. Soon Kat was staring at the walls and lines that, until then, she'd only seen modelled in blueprints.

"This is as close as you got to the house?" Hale asked Gabrielle.

She chomped her gum. "You mean to *the fortress*? Seriously nice picking, guys."

"We didn't pick it," Kat reminded her.

"Whatever. The place has a fifteen-foot stone wall."

"We know," Kat told her.

"Four perimeter towers. With guards."

"We know." Kat rolled her eyes.

"And a moat. Did you know that, Miss Smarty-pants? Did you know there's an actual moat? Like with *things* under the water?" Gabrielle gave a whole-body shiver (and parts of her shivered a bit more than others), but the point was clear.

Hale put the pictures back into his pocket and turned, placed his elbows on top of the wall, leaning there.

"Fine," Kat said. "What about the police report?" she asked, but Gabrielle just laughed. "You didn't check with the police...at all? You didn't ask them about...anything?" Kat asked over the sound of laughter that echoed on the cobblestones. Even Hale was smiling. But Kat just stood there, amazed that someone who shared Uncle Eddie's blood might not know that very few jobs in history have ever stayed off the police's radar entirely.

After all, people tended to notice if, at 8:02 pm,

every car alarm in the city went off for twenty minutes. Or if fifteen traffic lights went out between the hours of nine and ten. Or if a patrol car found an unmarked van abandoned by the side of the road – full of duct tape and hummingbirds.

These are the footprints of people who are very careful where they step. But they're footprints nonetheless.

"Men like Arturo Taccone don't call the police, Kat." Gabrielle spoke slowly, as if Kat had become amazingly stupid while she was away. "Those of us who don't abandon our families are able to learn these things."

"Geez, I left for a few—"

"You *left*." Gabrielle's voice was colder than the wind. "And you'd still be behind your ivy-covered walls if we hadn't…You'd still be there."

Authenticity is a strange thing, Kat knew. Someone carves an image out of stone. A machine prints a dead president on a bill. An artist puts paint on a canvas. Does it really matter who the painter is? Is a forged Picasso any less beautiful than a real one? Maybe it was just her, but Kat didn't think so. And still, as she looked between her cousin and Hale, she thought she smelled a fake.

"Gabrielle," Kat said slowly, "how'd you know there was ivy at Colgan?"

Kat heard her cousin scoff and make up some line

86

about a lucky guess. But an image was already flashing through Kat's mind: a grainy surveillance video. Someone in a hooded sweatshirt running across the quad. She turned to Hale and realized that he was too tall, too broad. The person on the screen had been close enough to Kat's size to fool the Colgan School Honour Board, but what really bothered Kat was that she had been tricked too.

"*Gabrielle*, Hale?" Kat smacked his shoulder. "It wasn't bad enough that you got me kicked out of school, but you had to use *her* to help you? Gabrielle!"

"I can hear you," her cousin sang beside her.

Hale looked at Gabrielle and gestured at Kat. "She's adorable when she's jealous." Kat kicked his shin. "Hey! It had to be done, remember? And contrary to popular belief, I don't know that many girls." They both stared at him. "OK, I don't know that many girls who have your special skills."

Gabrielle batted her eyelashes. "Oh, you do know how to make a girl feel special."

But Kat...Kat felt like a fool.

She looked at Hale. "I'll see you at the hotel." She turned to her cousin. "And I'll see you at Christmas or at one of your mother's weddings or...something. Thanks for coming, Gabrielle. But I'm sure there's a beach somewhere that wishes you were on it, so I'll let you get back to your business and I'll get back to mine."

She had almost made it to the corner when her cousin called, "You think you're the only person in the world who loves your dad?"

Kat stopped and studied Gabrielle. For the first time in her life, she could have sworn her cousin wasn't trying to con her. By the time Gabrielle was seven, she had been trained to call five different men daddy. There was an oil tycoon from Texas, a billionaire from Brazil, a man with a very unfortunate overbite who did something for the Paraguayan government, which oversaw the import/export of a highly overpriced fake Monet or two, but none of them had been her father.

"You need me," Gabrielle said. There was no doubt in her voice. No flirt. No ditz. She was in every way Uncle Eddie's great-niece. A pro. A con. A thief. "Like it or not, Kitty Kat, the reunion starts now."

Kat sat quietly as Gabrielle parked a tiny European car on the side of a winding country road. There were no headlights, no sounds. As Kat opened the door and stepped outside, she felt a cool damp breeze, and looked up at a dark starless sky. A thief couldn't ask for anything more.

"Tell me again why *I* had to ride in the backseat." Hale

stretched and stared down at her.

"The billionaire always rides in the back, big guy." She reached to pat him on the chest, but before she could pull away, he caught her wrist and held her gloved hand against his pounding heart.

"Are you sure this is a good idea?" he asked.

There were a million lies Kat could have told, but none more powerful than the truth. "This is our only idea."

While Gabrielle unlatched the bonnet and disabled the engine so that no roaming guards or passing busybodies would stop to ask questions, Kat kept her gaze locked with Hale's. In that moment, he looked a lot like the boy in the Superman pajamas. Scared but determined, and maybe just a little bit heroic.

"Kat, I—"

"Coming?" Gabrielle's whisper sliced through the night, cutting off whatever Hale was about to say. Kat was left with no choice but to turn and start up the steep embankment, shrouded in inky darkness, fallen branches sounding like firecrackers as they snapped underfoot.

"Oops," Kat said ten minutes later, stumbling for what felt like the millionth time. She didn't know what was worse, that Hale had had to steady her, or that Gabrielle was witnessing her clumsiness.

She kept waiting for her cousin to say *Kat's out of practice*. She was sure Hale was about to joke that the Colgan School's physical education curriculum was sorely lacking in practical application. But no one said a word as they made their way to the top of a tall hill, climbing steadily until Gabrielle came to a sudden stop. Kat almost collided with her cousin as she pointed and said, "That's it."

Even at night, even from this distance, anyone could see that Arturo Taccone's home was really a palace made of stone and wood, surrounded by vineyards and olive trees. A postcard paradise. But what Kat noticed were the guards and the towers, the walls and the gates. It was no paradise – it was more like a prison.

The grass was damp against their stomachs as the three of them lay at the top of the hill, looking down on the villa below. Kat hated to admit it, but Gabrielle was absolutely right: you did have to see it to believe it. The day before, when they had spread out the blueprints for Simon to study, Kat had thought Arturo Taccone's home was one of the hardest targets she'd ever seen. But when the dark clouds parted for a moment, and the moon shone like a spotlight on the moat, Kat realized that only a fool would approach those walls.

"Groundhog?" Hale asked.

"No time," Kat replied. "The tunnelling alone would take days, and Taccone wouldn't leave these woods unpatrolled for that long."

"Fallen Angel?"

"Maybe," Kat answered, looking to the sky. "But even on a night with no moon, that inner courtyard is awfully small to risk someone seeing you or your parachute. And no one builds guard towers if they aren't going to fill them with guards."

"With guns," Gabrielle added.

Kat watched her cousin turn onto her back, rest her head on her arms, and stare up at the black clouds that filled the sky. She might as well have been lying on a beach or in her own bed for all the ease she exhibited. But Kat's feet ached from the run through the woods. Her black ski cap was too tight and itchy. Kat was wondering what exactly it was that Hale smelled like, and whether or not she liked it.

Kat didn't know how to rob Arturo Taccone.

So Kat didn't know how *anyone* could have robbed Arturo Taccone.

And that was what she hated most of all.

"So someone either Trojan Horsed or Avon Ladied or..." Hale was going on, still listing options, but Kat was through speculating; she didn't dare to guess. Instead, she was recalling the words Hale had said to Simon: *It's not an ordinary job.* Kat was realizing that maybe it couldn't be done by an ordinary thief.

It was as if some invisible hand had taken hold of Kat in that moment – was pulling her up by the back of her black jacket, bringing her to her feet.

"Get down!" Gabrielle snapped, reaching for her cousin, but Kat was already moving to the edge of the ridge.

"Where are you going?" Hale asked as she walked purposefully towards the drawbridge, trying to shut down the part of her mind that asked *Drawbridge?*

"Kat!" Gabrielle hissed. "You're going to get caught."

The smile Kat flashed over her shoulder was almost wicked. "I know."

The gates loomed taller as Kat approached. Lights shone strategically around the perimeter, highlighting the drops of rain that were starting to slice through the black sky. Still, Kat walked slowly, deliberately, across the fields and towards the villa walls. She felt the stare of the security cameras. She sensed the movement of the guards. To keep her mind occupied, she tried to guess the age of the villa, the names of the original owners, the history of the lake. She tried to focus on the falling rain, her frizzing hair.

But mostly she tried to look calm as she strolled to the small metal box on the side of the road. She prayed her voice wouldn't betray her as she stared into the small camera and announced into the speaker, "My name is Katarina Bishop." Lightning struck behind her. "I'm here to see Arturo Taccone."

NINE

If the Taccone villa was a place that typically did not receive guests, it did not show it.

The man who opened the door reminded Kat oddly of Marcus, the way he wordlessly took her wet coat and softly asked her to follow. There were marble floors and chandeliers, fresh flowers, and fires burning in two of the four rooms she passed. But there were no stacks of mail lying on tables, no coats or scarves hung carelessly on the backs of chairs. It was a place that valued beauty and order in equal measure, Kat knew. So she stayed quiet, following her guide towards a set of double doors more intimidating than the drawbridge. She stood silent, waiting for an audience with Arturo Taccone.

He was sitting behind an antique desk when the doors opened, near another roaring fire in a room much like the study of the Hale family's upstate home. There were books and decanters, tall windows and a grand piano that Kat guessed he frequently played. Though the house was at least twenty thousand square feet, Kat had an inkling that this was the room where the man of the house really lived.

"Leave us," he ordered Kat's guide. She heard the double doors close behind her and knew that it was at least a little bit foolish not to tremble at being left alone with him. And yet her hands stayed steady. Her pulse didn't race.

"I should welcome you to my home, Katarina," he told her, tipping his head slightly. "I must say, this is a surprise. And I like to consider myself someone who is not easily surprised."

"Well," Kat said slowly, "I was in the mood for spaghetti."

Taccone smiled. "And you've come here alone," he said, but it was really a question.

"Now, I could say yes, and have you think I'm lying." She took a step forwards, ran her hand across the baby-soft leather of a wingback chair. "Or I could say no, and have you think I'm bluffing. So maybe I'll just say...no comment."

He pushed back from his desk as he studied her. "So you have – as you Americans say – backup?"

"Not really."

"But you're not afraid, are you?"

She was in Arturo Taccone's favourite room, but in

every way that really mattered, Kat was back on her home turf. "No. I guess I'm not."

He stared at her. After an excruciating pause, he asked, "Perhaps you don't think I'd hurt a little girl?"

For reasons Taccone would never understand, Kat was surprised at the words. It was strange to hear herself referred to in such a way. *Little*, she supposed she couldn't deny. But *girl* was odd. Woman or lady wouldn't have been any better. She had simply been so long inside boys' clubs that she forgot sometimes that, anatomically at least, she was not a younger, smaller version of the men who sat around Uncle Eddie's kitchen table. That she was, from a biological standpoint, very much like Gabrielle.

"That's a lovely piece," Kat said, pointing at a Louis XV armoire near the fireplace.

The man raised his eyebrows. "Did you come to steal it?"

"Darn it," Kat said with a snap of her fingers. "I knew I should have brought my big purse."

Scary men do scary things, but for Kat, nothing was as terrifying as the sound of Arturo Taccone laughing. "It's a shame we didn't meet under different circumstances, Katarina. I think I would have enjoyed knowing you. But we did not." He stood and walked to a cabinet, poured himself a glass of something that looked very old and expensive. "I take it that you do not have my paintings."

"That's kind of been my story all along."

"If you've come here to ask for more time, then—"

"Like I told your boys in Vegas, I'm working on it." She glared at Goon 2, who had slipped inside and was standing like a statue by the door. "Or didn't you get the message?"

"Yes, yes." He took a seat on the leather sofa in the centre of the room. "You have indeed been making some interesting inquiries. Your great-uncle's home in New York…that, I could understand. Your uncle is the sort of man who should be consulted. But the trip to Las Vegas" – he leaned back and took a sip – "that came as a surprise. And then I learned that we had visitors this evening. Well, you can understand if I'm perplexed."

"I told you everything in Paris," Kat explained, her voice steady. "My father didn't steal your paintings. With a little time and a little help, I may be able to tell you who did. I may even be able to arrange for them to be returned—"

His smile widened. "Now *that* is an interesting proposition."

"But first…"

"Help?" the man guessed.

She nodded. "You say my father did this."

"I *know* he did this."

"How?"

"Oh, Katarina, surely any half-decent thief would know that I have taken...*precautions*...to protect myself and my belongings." Arturo Taccone raised a hand, waved at the opulent surroundings.

"The Stig 360," she said with a smile. "Nice. Personally, I prefer the cameras in the 340 models. They're clunkier, but they have more range."

Outside the villa, the rain was falling in torrents, but inside, Taccone's voice was as dry as kindling. "I had hoped you would take my word that your father has done this terrible thing, Katarina. But if—"

"Look." Kat's voice was sharper than she'd thought possible as she stepped closer to the man at the centre of the room. Goon 2 made a move towards her, but Taccone stopped him with a wave. "It's not a pride thing. Or a trust thing. It's an information thing. You're a man who makes careful decisions based on the best information possible, are you not, Signor Taccone?"

"Of course."

"Then help me. Help me get your paintings back. You've got proof, you say?"

Taccone held his drink to the light as if toasting Kat and her courage. "Of course."

Kat smiled, but her expression held no cheer. "Then show me what you've got."

There would come a time – although Kat didn't know it yet – when her conversation with Taccone that evening would be told and retold around Uncle Eddie's kitchen table a thousand times. When the story of her crossing the drawbridge would involve not rain but bullets; when the tale of her asking Arturo Taccone for his help would include threats and windows and something involving a pair of antique duelling pistols (which, according to legend, Kat would also steal).

But Kat herself never told the story. Hale and Gabrielle lay in the darkness, staring down at the grounds when the drawbridge lowered and Kat left of her own free will, taking her sweet time.

As she walked through the rain and darkness, Hale and Gabrielle didn't notice the way she kept the small disc from Arturo Taccone tucked under her arm. But, of course, they would see it eventually.

And, of course, eventually, it would change everything.

TEN

The hotel suite was nice. Hale (or, more specifically, Marcus) didn't know how to reserve any other kind. The sofa was plush, and the television was large, but as Kat settled in to watch the disc Taccone had given her, she was anything but comfortable.

"There should be popcorn," Gabrielle's voice cut through the suite. "Am I the only one who thinks there should be popcorn?"

Kat pulled her dry sweater around her and tried to tell herself it was the rain and her damp hair that had chilled her.

"Milk Duds," Hale said as he sank to the end of the sofa. "I, personally, am a fan of the Dud." And Kat suddenly realized where the chill was coming from.

Hale hadn't spoken to her in the car or looked at her in the lift. Kat pulled a notebook from her bag and crossed her legs, wondering if Hale would ever forgive her for walking away from him. Again.

She reached for the remote control and pushed PLAY. The television flickered. Ghostly black-and-white images flashed across the screen: the long entryway that she had walked down only an hour before, a professional-grade kitchen, a wine cellar, a billiards parlour, Arturo Taccone's private study. And finally...

"Stop."

Gabrielle hit the PAUSE button, and the image froze on a room that Kat hadn't seen – a room Kat could only assume very few people *ever* saw.

A bench was the only piece of furniture. The floors were solid stone instead of marble or wood. But the most remarkable thing was the five paintings that hung on the far wall.

"Blueprints," she said, but Hale was already rolling the spare set of documents onto the coffee table between the sofa and the TV.

"Here." Kat pointed to a room on the plans that had the same dimensions as the one on the screen. "Looks like it's located underground, probably only accessible here." She tapped the blueprints. "A hidden lift in Taccone's office."

"How do you know that?" Gabrielle asked.

Kat thought about the dark wooden panelling behind

Taccone's desk. "Because I'm pretty sure I was standing right in front of it tonight."

Hale tensed beside her, but he didn't speak as he touched the remote. The black-and-white images played like an old silent movie without a star, until the video flickered back to Taccone's office.

Floor-to-ceiling windows dominated one wall, so it was easy to see the bolt of lightning that flashed through the sky on the screen in front of them. A split second later, the screen went black. Kat could imagine the villa going dark, someone complaining about ancient wiring and a dislike of storms

But in the suite, all Kat heard was the deep sighs of her companions and their simultaneous exclamation, *"Benjamin Franklin."*

Having done it herself on more than one occasion, it wasn't hard for Kat to imagine the thief scouting the old villa and formulating a plan. She imagined him taking a room in town – something that catered to tourists, perhaps. A place where he could be just another visitor to the countryside, while he watched and waited for a stormy night.

When the tape resumed, Kat leaned close and squinted. "How long until the generators kicked on?"

"Forty-five seconds," Gabrielle answered.

"Not bad," Hale said.

"For Taccone's system or our guy?" Gabrielle asked.

He shrugged as if to say it was a toss-up.

"Everything else went black, but this room…" Kat pointed to the vaultlike space that filled the screen. "This room must be on a separate feed from the rest of the house. *This room* kept recording." Kat glanced from the screen to the blueprints. "Looks like it's directly under…"

But her voice trailed off as, on screen, water began dripping from the gallery ceiling.

"The moat," they all finished in unison.

"Cool." Hale's voice was pure awe. "Benjamin Franklin with a side of Loch Ness Monster."

"Eww!" Gabrielle exclaimed. "That moat is disgusting. Seriously. No way would I go near it."

"From what I could see, there were at least five Old Masters in that room, Gabs," Hale said. "You'd go near it."

"Maybe," Gabrielle admitted. "But if he cut a hole in the ceiling of a room under a *moat*, then why isn't it flooded?"

Kat turned away, not needing to see the screen to know what was happening. "He rode a mini-submarine in from the lake and then sealed it to the room's roof. After that, all he had to do was open the hatch, cut the hole, and… A *mini-submarine*," Kat said again with a shake of her head, as if trying to cast aside a terrible case of déjà vu.

Her cousin looked at her. "How do you know?"

"Because that's what Dad did." A silence fell over them as Kat stood and walked to the windows that overlooked the quiet streets. "Two years ago. Venice. It was—"

"Beautiful," Hale said, but Kat had another word in mind.

"Risky."

"Well," Hale said slowly, "at least now we know why your dad is Taccone's leading suspect."

"*Only* suspect," Gabrielle corrected.

On the screen, a masked man in a plain black wet suit was easing through the fresh hole in the gallery roof, moving with silent purpose. There were no hurried or wasted steps as he neutralized the pressure switches on the individual paintings and removed them from the wall, packed each carefully in a watertight case, and slid them through the hole in the ceiling and into the craft Kat knew was waiting in the moat outside.

"Taccone said that when the power went out, someone looped the video feed to the guard's station, so no one saw a thing. What we're watching is from an off-site backup system that our guy either didn't know about or missed." Kat shrugged. "However it happened, no one even knew those paintings were gone until Taccone got home from a business trip."

"What kind of business *is* he in?" Gabrielle asked.

"The business of being incredibly scary," Kat answered at the same time Hale simply said, "Evil."

The girls looked at him. When he spoke again, his voice was soft. "Arturo Taccone is in the business of evil."

Something about the way he turned back to the TV told Kat there was something he wasn't telling her – information obtained from private investigators or corporate gossips, from Manhattan socialites or high-ranking Italian officials. They were the kinds of stories told in smoke-filled rooms over expensive Cuban cigars.

But some stories make your hands shake. Sometimes too many details make you fidget in the dark. So Kat didn't ask Hale to tell the tales. She looked at him, watched him toss the remote on the table and say, "So maybe I'm going to handcuff myself to you the next time you decide to take a stroll."

"I was fine," Kat insisted, desperate for him to understand. "He...likes me. I amuse him. He thinks I'm" – Kat hadn't realized until now – "like him."

"You're not," Hale blurted. For the first time in hours he looked into her eyes. "You are *not* like Arturo Taccone."

There were times when Kat thought she knew

everything there was to know about W. W. Hale the Fifth – with the single exception of his first name – and then there were times like this, when she felt that he was like one of the first edition novels in the library of his upstate house: she hadn't even finished the first chapter.

"How deep would the river that runs to the moat be at its shallowest?" Gabrielle asked.

Kat shrugged. "Eight feet?"

Hale nodded. "I'd say ten at the most."

"How small would the sub have to be?" Gabrielle asked.

"Small," Kat answered.

"Note to self," Gabrielle said. "When it comes to moats, deeper isn't necessarily better."

Then Hale asked, "*How* small?"

Kat heard the hum of a motorcycle on the street below, saw lights shining on the Coliseum in the distance. In the dim hotel room, a masked man stood frozen on the TV screen, caught in the act of stealing five priceless paintings and her father's future.

"There's one way to find out."

10 DAYS
UNTIL DEADLINE

NAPLES,
ITALY

ELEVEN

The Mariano & Sons Dive Shop in Naples was a family-run affair and very proud of that particular fact. Mariano the Second had been the son of a fisherman, but he'd suffered from an unfortunate tendency towards seasickness and was forced to find a respectable career that could be safely conducted on dry land. So he built boats.

Mariano the Third built bigger boats.

And by the time a girl from a very different type of family business arrived at their shopfront on the Mediterranean coast, Mariano the Fourth had built and patented at least half a dozen of the most advanced (and justifiably expensive) watercrafts in the world.

Or so Kat's father had told her right before he'd made a trip to Venice.

As soon as the receptionist at Il Negozio di Mariano & Figli saw the young man strolling through the double glass doors, she could tell he was from money – that almost anything in their showroom was something for which he could simply write a chedue. Maybe pay cash. Certainly charge on whatever ridiculously high-limit credit card he carried.

But that wasn't why she smiled when the young man removed his sunglasses, leaned across the sleek glass counter, and said, "*Ciao*." The woman felt as if every muscle in her body were starting to melt. "I was wondering if you could help me."

Running a crew means delegating, knowing when to sit out and let others take the lead. Understanding what your best resources are and exactly how to use them. But as Kat stood across the busy seaside street, watching the young receptionist flirt with Hale, she began to worry that Hale might leave with a girlfriend and not a name.

The lack of a name worried her. The presence of a girlfriend, she assured herself, did not.

For ten minutes she stood outside, watching the scene through the large picture window. Hands brushed against shoulders. Eyelashes batted up and down. The whole spectacle was enough to make Kat pace (although every good thief knows she's far less likely to be noticed if she stays perfectly still).

"Are you watching this?" she asked Gabrielle for the

fourth time. But her cousin's attentions were focused on the young man at the pavement café who was equally enamoured by Gabrielle and, more specifically, her highly inadequate skirt.

"He's gonna blow it." Kat threw her hands in the air. "It's our one good lead and he's gonna blow it."

But her cousin didn't notice. If she had, she might have said something – done something – but as it was, she didn't even turn until Kat was across the street, walking through the gleaming doors.

"There you are." Kat was panting, only half pretending to be out of breath as she walked up to the counter.

"Hi." Hale pulled away from the salesgirl's hand as if he had felt a spark. Literally. "I was just..." he started.

Kat sighed. "Dad says you have thirty minutes to make it back on board or else we're leaving for Majorca without you and telling your mother you fell overboard." Kat turned to the salesgirl. "Of course, I voted for actually pushing him overboard." She exhaled loudly. "I'm his sister."

"*Step*sister," Hale added without missing a beat.

The young woman smiled with the knowledge that Kat wasn't his girlfriend. Kat wasn't competition. She was simply a petite girl who was too pale and too thin to have spent much time on the Italian coast.

"Are you almost finished?" Kat asked with some genuine annoyance.

"Yeah," Hale said, sounding exactly like the bored billionaire he was. "They've got some cool stuff."

Somehow Kat doubted that the geniuses behind the finest watercrafts in the world would like to hear their inventions demoted to "cool stuff," but if the salesgirl shared this feeling, she didn't show it.

"So are you going to buy one or aren't you?" Kat asked.

"Uh…yeah," Hale said, walking around the showroom. "I kinda like this one."

If Kat hadn't known better, she might have thought the vessel Hale had chosen was a model, a replica – something shrunk down to size in order to fit onto the showroom floor. But, of course, it wasn't. And that, of course, was the point.

The *Sirena Royal* was the smallest non-military under-water vessel in the world. Not much larger than the mermaids for which it was named, it was six feet long and four feet tall, roughly the size of a go-cart – the very type of craft that could submerge in the small river that connected to the Taccone moat. The very type of craft that – at this moment – was their one and only lead.

"Yeah," Hale said, standing back and admiring it. "I'll take this one."

"*Eccellente, signor!*" the salesgirl exclaimed, but Hale just jerked his head in Kat's direction.

"You've got the credit card, don't you, sis?"

Kat was more than happy to follow the young woman to a tall counter, where she began pulling out forms and shuffling papers until Kat's pale hand landed on top of her own, cutting her off in midmotion.

"If I may be honest, Lucia," Kat said, reading the woman's name tag, "my dear stepbrother is a bored little boy." Kat looked at Hale from the corner of her eye. "He likes toys."

Kat could never be sure if Hale had heard her or not, but nevertheless, he chose that moment to pick up a model of a world-class racing yacht and begin making bubble noises as it dove to the bottom of an imaginary lake.

"Three years ago he convinced his mother to buy a villa on Lake Como because he needed a place to play." Kat paused for a moment, recalling that Hale's family did have a home in Northern Italy. "The year after that he bought an eighty-foot yacht because he needed something to play *on*."

Behind her, Hale was using his model to dive-bomb a cup full of pencils.

Kat leaned closer to the salesgirl and lowered her voice. "But boys don't like sharing their toys, do they, Lucia?"

The salesgirl shook her head. "No."

"And so when the Bernard brothers bought a *ninety-foot* yacht last summer, my dear stepbrother was not very happy. And" – she cut her eyes back to Hale and lowered her voice to a conspiratorial whisper – "unfortunately, when he's not happy, his mother isn't happy, and when his mother isn't happy…"

Lucia nodded. "I see. Yes."

"I'm telling you this because he really needs to be *the* guy with the *Sirena Royal* – not *one of* the guys with the *Sirena Royal*." Kat flashed her most sympathetic smile. "Trust me, if we get home and find out that there's another one just across the—"

"Oh no, there isn't!" Lucia exclaimed.

"Really?" Kat asked.

"Well, to be honest…" Lucia stole a glance around the room, as if what she was about to say might make three generations of Marianos roll over in their graves. "It's really more for show, you know? We don't sell that many."

In the corner of the room, Hale had strapped himself inside the *Sirena Royal* and was doing his best imitation of a World War II fighter pilot, bombing unsuspecting foes.

"But they're so cool," Kat said. "I find that hard to believe."

"Really," Lucia soothed. "In the last year, we sell only two."

"I knew it!" Kat said, throwing up her hands and starting towards Hale. "I told my brother that the Bernard brothers would already have—"

"Oh no, miss," Lucia said. "We no sell them to brothers."

"Really?" Kat turned. "Are you certain?"

"Oh yes. The first went to a business. They do the studies underwater. It's really quite—"

"And the other?" Kat asked, stepping closer.

"Well, he was someone who might run in the same... *circles* as your family," Lucia admitted carefully, but Kat thought, *You have no idea.*

She watched the young woman shift as if debating what to say or, more precisely, how to say it. Finally, she whispered, "This man...you see, he was quite...*wealthy.*"

"Well then, I'm afraid..." Kat said, turning to walk away, counting on Lucia's eventual...

"But he didn't live in Italy!"

Kat turned slowly. "Oh, really?"

"Oh, yes. Mr Romani."

"Romani?" Kat asked.

"Yes," the young woman said. "Visily Romani. He was very specific – he wanted his *Sirena* delivered to Austria."

"Austria?"

"Yes, directly to one of his estates. Near Vienna."

* * *

Although she would never have admitted it out loud, there were many things Katarina Bishop had begun to like about the Colgan School.

There was, after all, something to be said for sleeping in the same bed every night and always knowing the way to and from the bathroom in the dark. She'd absolutely adored the library – an entire building where anyone could take things they didn't own and feel no remorse about it. But the thing Kat had loved most about Colgan – the thing she missed most as she sat beside Hale and Gabrielle on a train bound for Vienna – was that one of the most strenuous prep schools in the world was the only place Kat had ever been where it was OK not to think.

After all, on her very first day at Colgan she'd been given a piece of paper that told her what classes she would attend and at what times. There was a board in the main hall that announced what meals she would eat and what sporting events she could witness. Each week her teachers dutifully told her which chapters she should read and from which books, which projects she should perform and in what order.

It was exactly as she'd suspected ever since the night Uncle Vinnie (who wasn't really her uncle) had pulled her out of Uncle Eddie's kitchen and informed her that boarding school would be a lot like prison (which, ironically, was exactly where Vinnie had been before turning up on Uncle Eddie's front porch that very night).

Kat had listened to him with a clarity that suited Uncle Eddie's great-niece. She didn't let it scare her. She just analyzed all the angles and came to the conclusion that Uncle Vinnie was exactly right, and she essentially had two options: Colgan now or jail later.

Colgan had cuter uniforms.

But now autumn was over and Colgan was gone; Kat was left to stare out the train window at the snowy caps of the Alps. In her coat pocket she had three passports and one of Hale's credit cards. She was very good with four languages and decent at two more. She could go anywhere. She could do anything. Maybe it was the altitude, but suddenly Kat felt herself growing dizzy – short on air and smothered by the infinite possibilities that lay before her, and the questions her mind couldn't help but ask.

Like, how was it possible for Gabrielle to be even prettier when she slept, when Kat herself could rarely wake up without encountering at least a little bit of drool?

And why did Gabrielle insist on sleeping with her head on Hale's shoulder, when Kat – who had hit him there on a number of occasions – knew for a fact that it was quite hard and the compartment above the seats contained an assortment of very soft pillows?

Kat tried not to think about the other things – the hard questions that were locked outside, racing the train. She wished she could outrun them, lose them like a tail. But Kat knew better. They'd be waiting for her in Austria.

Kat's ears popped as the train went faster, climbed higher, and the thoughts that had been swirling in her mind narrowed to one person, one place.

Visily Romani.

Vienna, Austria.

And with that, Kat closed her eyes. She didn't see the first flakes of snow fall outside her window. She didn't feel Hale cover her with a blanket. She was already fast asleep.

9 DAYS
UNTIL DEADLINE

VIENNA,
AUSTRIA

TWELVE

The one thought that Kat hadn't had on the train was the first one that torpedoed her mind as soon as they reached the station the next morning: sometimes it's nice being partnered with a billionaire.

"Did you have a nice trip, miss?" Marcus asked, appearing from thin air on the crowded platform. Their bags were already on the cart in front of him. When they stepped outside, Kat was struck by the frigid air, but thankfully a car was already waiting.

The winter's first snow had been ploughed neatly to the side of the roads, and the pavements were covered with tourists and townspeople going about their day. Kat watched through her window and thought: *Visily Romani could be here.*

Visily Romani could be anywhere.

Visily Romani could be anyone.

No one spoke on the car ride or said a word as they

walked through the hotel lobby. Kat had the vague realization that it was nice reaching a penthouse via a lift and not a ventilation duct, and as the car rose, she closed her eyes. She might have been content to stand like that all day. All week. All year. But too soon the doors were sliding open.

And Kat was listening to a deep voice say, "Hello, Katarina."

Kat had heard of the presidential suite at Das Palace Hotel in Vienna, of course. Every self-respecting thief was aware that this room was traditionally used for hosting kings and princes, presidents and CEOs. But for all its history, the most intimidating thing about the room right then was the sight of Uncle Eddie, standing beside a roaring fire.

"Welcome to Vienna."

When Uncle Eddie held out his arms, Gabrielle rushed into them, gushing at him in rapid Russian. No one translated for Hale, but he understood the exchange. Four days ago, Kat had walked back into her uncle's home and his graces, but anyone could see that Gabrielle, who had spent the last six months using cleavage and quick hands to pick some of the plusher pockets on the Riviera, had never really left the family kitchen.

"Your mother?" Uncle Eddie asked, holding Gabrielle at arm's length.

"Engaged," Gabrielle said with a sigh.

Uncle Eddie nodded as if he'd heard it all before. "He has art?"

"Jewels," Gabrielle said. "Family stuff. He's a count."

"Or a duke," Hale chimed in.

"I get them confused," Gabrielle confessed.

"Who doesn't?" Uncle Eddie admitted with a shrug, still holding her and beaming. "It's good to see you, little one." He scanned her short skirt. "I only wish I were not seeing quite so much of you."

Gabrielle didn't even register the insult. "It's good to see you too. But how did you—"

Uncle Eddie shook his head. The question wasn't *how* her uncle had got there. The question, Kat knew, was *what had he come to tell them?* What had he learned that he couldn't share over the phone? And what was she going to have to do about it?

He settled into the chair closest to the fire and looked up at Kat. "You have been to see Signor Mariano?"

Kat was faintly aware of the smell of good coffee, and noticed that at some point a china cup had appeared in Uncle Eddie's hand. But her attention, like Hale's and Gabrielle's, was entirely absorbed by Uncle Eddie.

"Visily Romani." He was speaking to them all, but Kat felt her uncle's gaze settle upon her. "This name is not unfamiliar to you?"

"Is it an alias?" Kat asked.

"Of course." He smiled as if enjoying the notion that she might still be, in part, a little girl.

"And the shipping address here in Austria?" Hale asked.

"You have indeed been busy." Uncle Eddie chuckled but quickly grew serious. "I only wish it were not for nothing."

"Who is he?" Kat asked.

"He is no one." Uncle Eddie's eyes passed to Gabrielle. "He is everyone."

Uncle Eddie was not a man of riddles, and so Kat knew the words must matter, but she couldn't fathom how.

"I...I don't understand," she said with a shake of her head.

"It's a Chelovek Pseudonima, Katarina," her uncle said, and Gabrielle drew a quick breath. Kat blinked against the fire's glare. Outside, the snow fell softly, and yet it felt to Kat as if all of Austria were standing still – as if nothing could ever break the trance until –

"What's a Chelovek Pseudonima?"

Kat looked at Hale and blinked, somehow managed to remember that despite being fluent in the language of the thief, he would never be a native speaker. A member of the family.

"What?" Hale's voice rose in frustration. "What's wrong? What is a Chelovek Pseudo—"

"Alias Man," Gabrielle whispered. "A Chelovek Pseudonima is an Alias Man."

But the literal translation was lost on Hale. Kat read it in his eyes, saw it in his impatient hands.

"The old families..." Kat said, staring at him. "They had names – aliases – that they only used when they were doing things that were too big, too dangerous – things they had to keep hidden...even from each other. They were secret names, Hale. *Sacred names.*"

Kat looked at her uncle. She guessed that in all of his years he had rarely seen a Pseudonima used. If Kat had asked to hear the stories, her uncle might have told her that Visily Romani had once stolen some highly incriminating documents from a czar, and a diamond from a queen. He'd smuggled Nazi war plans out of Germany and done a fair amount of work behind the Iron Curtain. But Uncle Eddie offered no such details.

Instead, he looked at the next generation and smiled with the irony of it as he explained, "If Visily Romani were real, he would be four hundred years old and the greatest thief who'd ever lived."

Hale looked at each one of them in turn. "I still don't understand."

"It is an alias that is not used lightly, young man," Uncle Eddie answered. Kat knew the words were really for her. "It is a name that is not used by simply *anyone*."

Uncle Eddie rose from his chair. "This is finished, Katarina." He walked towards the door as if there were something on his stove that needed stirring. "I will tell your father. I will try to make amends with Mr Taccone."

"But—" Gabrielle was on her feet.

"A Pseudonima is a sacred thing!" Her uncle whirled. "Any job done in the name of Visily Romani will not be undone by children!"

In a way, every thief Kat knew was a child at heart, and she merely had the body that matched – a body that could be utilized in very effective ways if the air ducts were small or the guards were naive. But she'd never been spoken to like she was a little girl.

Her uncle stopped at the door. Marcus was there, waiting silently with his coat.

"You may go back to school if you wish, Katarina." Uncle Eddie put on his hat as the butler reached for the door. "I'm afraid this is beyond even you now."

THIRTEEN

Kat didn't watch her uncle go. She stayed seated on the sofa, vaguely aware of Gabrielle saying something about spending the winter working the ski chalets in Switzerland. She realized at some point that Hale had sent Marcus out for food. She was wondering briefly how he could eat at a time like this, when he turned to her and said, "Well?"

Kat thought she heard Gabrielle talking on the phone in one of the bedrooms, explaining that she might be arriving in town and "Oh, Sven, you are a flirt..."

But Uncle Eddie's voice was still echoing in Kat's ears – *It is beyond even you now* – resounding with the things he did not say.

Someone very, very good had gone after Taccone's paintings.

Someone very, very connected had known enough to call into play one of the oldest rules of their world.

Someone very, very greedy had allowed her father to stay alone in Taccone's spotlight.

Only someone very, very foolish would disobey Uncle Eddie and try to do something about it now.

That is, if there was anything left to do.

"You know we could always…" Hale started, but Kat was already up, already moving towards the door.

"I'll be back…" She stopped and studied Hale. The look in his eyes told her that if her father's safety were something he could have purchased, he would have written her a cheque, sold his Monet, his Bentley, his soul. She wanted to thank him, to ask why someone like him would choose to be halfway around the world with someone like her.

But all she choked out was a pitiful, "I'll be back soon." And then she walked away, into the cold.

Kat wasn't sure how long she'd been gone, or where she was going. Hours passed. The surveillance video Arturo Taccone had given her played in a constant loop in her mind until, finally, she found herself in the doorway of a bakery. She savoured the smell of bread and realized that she was hungry. Then, just as suddenly, she realized she wasn't alone.

"If you die of pneumonia, I'm pretty sure there are at

least a dozen guys who'll try to kill me and make it look like an accident."

Kat studied Hale's reflection in the bakery window. He didn't smile. He didn't scold. He simply handed her a cup of hot chocolate and draped his heavy coat around her shoulders.

All around them, the snow was falling harder, covering the streets like a blanket – a fresh start. But Kat was an excellent thief; she knew not even an Austrian winter could help them hide their tracks.

She turned and looked up and down the street. A trolley car ran silently across a cobblestone square. Snowcapped mountains and ornate eighteenth century buildings stretched out in every direction, and Kat felt extraordinarily small in the shadows of the Alps. Especially young in a place so old.

"What do we do now, Hale?" Kat didn't want to cry. She willed her voice not to crack. "What do we do now?"

"Uncle Eddie said not to do anything." He placed his arm around her and steered her down the pavement. For a second, Kat felt that perhaps her legs had frozen; she'd forgotten how to move. "Do you trust Uncle Eddie?" he asked.

"Of course. He'd do anything for me."

Hale stopped. His breath was a foggy, fine mist. "What would he do for *your dad*?"

Sometimes it takes an outsider, someone with fresh eyes to see the truth. Standing there, Kat knew that was the question she should have been asking all along. She thought of Uncle Eddie's order and Arturo Taccone's cold eyes.

Arturo Taccone wasn't going to get his paintings back.

Arturo Taccone was never going to see his paintings again.

She brought the cocoa to her lips, but it was too hot. She stared into the swirls of chocolate as the snow fell into her cup, and, in her mind, the video kept playing.

"We're crazy," Hale said, shivering without his coat. He took her arm, tried to lead her into the shelter of a nearby café. But Kat stood staring at the snow as fat flakes melted into her steaming cocoa. Suddenly, she remembered a red door. She recalled playing among stacks of books and sitting quietly on her mother's lap.

"What is it?" Hale asked, stepping closer.

Kat closed her eyes and tried to pretend she was back at Colgan, taking a test. The answer was in a book she'd read, a lecture she'd heard – all she had to do was go into the vault of her mind and steal the truth that lay inside.

"Kat." Hale tried to break through her concentration. "I said—"

"Why doesn't Taccone go to the police?" she blurted.

Hale held his hands out as if the answer should be obvious. And it was. "He doesn't like the police. And he doesn't want them getting their nasty fingerprints all over his pretty pictures."

"But what if it's more than that?" she prompted. "Why keep them hidden under the moat? Why not have them insured? What if…"

"They aren't really *his*?"

Around them, shops were closing for the night. She looked at the darkened windows, still looking for the red door that was hundreds of miles away.

"Kat—"

"Warsaw." Church bells began to chime. "We need to go to Warsaw."

8 DAYS
UNTIL DEADLINE

WARSAW,
POLAND

FOURTEEN

Abiram Stein was not unaccustomed to teenagers arriving on his doorstep. Most were students, they'd tell him, there to search for a better grade somewhere among his rows of files and stacks of books. A few were treasure seekers, convinced that they had seen a misplaced Renoir or a Rembrandt tucked inside their grandmother's attic and were curious to know what – if any – finder's fee might be coming their way.

But when he woke to the sound of knocking that Monday morning, he pulled on his robe and moved through the dark house, completely unsure what he might find.

"*Wer ist da?*" he said, throwing open the door, expecting to have to squint against the light, but he had misgauged the time. The sun was still too low to shine over the book-shop across the road. "*Was wollen Sie? Es ist mal smach ehr früh,*" Mr Stein snapped in his native German.

The pair of teenagers standing on his porch wore backpacks like the students, and had nervous, hopeful eyes like the treasure hunters. But Mr Stein could not determine to which group they belonged. He only knew that his bed upstairs was warm and soft while that porch was cold and hard, and he was quite certain which one he preferred to see before the sun rose.

"Ich entschuldige mich für die Stunde, Herr Stein."

The girl spoke German with the faintest hint of an American accent. The boy didn't speak at all.

More than anything, Mr Stein wanted to close the door and go back upstairs, but something had taken a hold in him, a curiosity about this girl. And the boy, too, he supposed. Because, of all the backpacks and wide eyes he had seen on his small porch, none had ever come before the sun.

"You would prefer English, would you not?" he asked.

Kat had thought she was using her best German, but the man had placed her accent too easily. Colgan, she feared, might have taken more from her than she knew.

"I'm fine either way," the girl said, but Mr Stein nodded at the boy beside her.

"I believe your companion would not agree."

Hale yawned. His expression was vacant. And Kat remembered that despite the chauffeurs and private jets, there were some things even Hales could not buy, and a proper night's sleep was one of them.

"We're sorry for the hour, Mr Stein," Kat said, her (apparently rusty) German abandoned. "I'm afraid we've just arrived in Warsaw. We would have waited—"

"Then wait!" the man grumbled, starting to close the door.

He may have been sleepy, but Hale was still quick, and he silently leaned against the red door as if he simply needed a way to stay upright.

"I'm afraid we don't have the time to wait, sir," Kat said.

"My time is valuable too, *fräulein*. Almost as valuable as my rest."

"Of course," Kat said, glancing down. Despite the freezing wind, she pulled her black ski cap from her head. In the glass of the door's small window she saw her hair standing on end, felt the static coursing through her – a charge that had been building for days. She knew answers lay behind that red door. Not all. But some. And she feared that if she turned to walk away now, gripped the metal railing of the stairs, the charge might stop her heart.

"We have some questions, sir…about art." She paused, waiting, but the man merely stared at her with sleepy eyes. Behind him, rows of filing cabinets lined the wall in front of several windows, blocking out the early morning light. Stacks of papers ran through the space like a maze.

"Try the Smithsonian, pretty American girl," he said with a faint smile. "I'm just a crazy old man with too much time and too few friends."

"Sir, I was told that you could help me."

"By whom?" he snapped.

Hale looked at Kat as if he had the same question. Mr Stein stepped closer. The first rays of the sun were just peeking over the buildings across the street. They illuminated the features of a small girl with a mane of dark hair, and before she even spoke, he knew what her answer would be.

"My mother."

"You look like her," Abiram Stein said, handing Kat a cup of coffee. "You have been told this before, I suspect."

Kat had often wondered what was more cruel: to so closely resemble a mother who had left too soon, making you equal parts daughter and ghost, or to have nothing of your parent in your features – to be, aesthetically speaking, more than one generation removed. But Kat liked the way Mr Stein was looking at her. It was different from the way Uncle Eddie seemed to be measuring her against her mother as a thief. It was nothing like the moments when her father seemed startled by her, as if his eyes had mistaken her for his long-lost wife.

But when Mr Stein sipped his hot coffee and watched Kat drink hers, he smiled the way he might if he saw a replica of his favourite childhood toy in a shop window – happy that something he loved wasn't entirely gone from the world.

"I thought you might come to see me again someday," he said after a long silence.

Beside her, Hale was coming awake, taking in every aspect of Abiram Stein's cluttered existence. "Don't you have a computer?"

Mr Stein scoffed. Kat answered for him. "He *is* the computer."

Mr Stein eyed her again and nodded appreciatively.

"I manage to maintain a good deal of my research" – the older man tapped his head – "in safe places." He leaned on his cluttered desk. "But I have a feeling that my organizational systems are not why you're here."

"We were travelling and we had some questions—"

"About art," Mr Stein said with a roll of his hands, gesturing for Kat to get to the good stuff.

"And my mother always spoke highly of you."

"You remember your visit here?" he asked.

Kat nodded. "My cocoa was too hot, so you opened

a window and held the cup outside until it caught some snowflakes." She smiled at the memory. "I drove my parents crazy for a month after that, refusing to take anything but fresh snow in my hot chocolate."

Mr Stein looked as if he wanted to laugh but had forgotten how. "You were so little that day. And so much like your mother. You lost her too soon, Katarina," he said. "We. We all lost her too soon."

"Thank you. Your work was very important to her."

"And does your appearance here mean that you've made a discovery relevant to our work together?"

Kat shook her head. Hale shifted, and she felt his patience wane.

"Unfortunately, I'm here on another matter."

The man leaned back in his old wooden chair. "I see. And what sort of matter would this be?"

Hale glanced at Kat – a quick look with only one translation: *Can we trust him?* Her reply was a simple: *We have to.*

"The kind of matter my mother did when she *wasn't* researching here. With you."

Kat had wondered off and on for the past few hours how much of her mother's life Mr Stein knew about. But the answer, it turned out, was in Abiram Stein's eyes as he smiled. "I see."

"We need to know," Kat went on. "I need to know if these...*mean* anything to you."

Hale reached into his coat pocket and removed five sheets of paper. Five pictures – grainy images from odd angles captured from a piece of video footage. Mr Stein laid them across the cluttered desk and sat for a long time, whispering quietly in a language Kat didn't understand. For a moment she was sure he had forgotten that she and Hale were even in the room. He studied the images as if they were a deck of cards and he were a fortune-teller, trying to read his own fate.

"These..." he said finally. His voice was sharper as he demanded, "How? Where?"

"It's..." Kat stumbled when she realized she had finally met someone to whom she didn't know how to lie.

Fortunately, Hale never had that problem. "We saw a sort of home movie recently. Those were on it."

Mr Stein's eyes grew even wider. "They're together? All in one place?"

Hale nodded. "We think so. It's a collection we—"

"This is no collection!" Abiram Stein shouted. "They are prisoners of war."

Kat thought back to the room hidden beneath a moat, guarded by one of the best security systems in the world, and she knew that he was right. Arturo Taccone had taken five priceless pieces of history and locked them away until the night Visily Romani set them free.

"Do you know what this is, young man?" Mr Stein asked Hale, holding up a photo of a painting: a graceful young woman in a pale white dress stood behind a curtain, peering out at a stage.

"It looks like Degas," Hale answered.

"It is." Mr Stein nodded his approval of Kat's choice of companions. "It's called *Dancer Waiting in the Wings*." The man pushed himself out of his chair and crossed the room to a filing cabinet overrun with books and magazines and creeping plants that draped all the way to the dusty floor. He opened the drawer and removed a folder, brought it back to his desk.

"I presume you are a well-travelled young man," Mr Stein stated. "Tell me, have you seen that painting before?"

Hale shook his head.

"That is because *no one* has seen it in more than half a century." Mr Stein settled into his hard wooden seat as if he'd used all his energy crossing the room and no longer had the strength to stand. "Johan Schulhoff was a banker in a small but prosperous town near the Austrian border in 1938. He had a lovely daughter. A beautiful wife. A nice home."

Mr Stein opened the folder where a photocopy of a

family portrait was taped inside. It showed a family of three in their best clothes, smiling their best smiles, while *Dancer Waiting in the Wings* looked on from the wall behind them.

"This painting hung in their dining room until the day the Nazis came and took it – and every member of his family – away. None of them was ever seen again." He stared at the photo. Tears gathered in his eyes as he whispered, "Until now."

Kat thought of her mother, who had sat in this very chair and sifted through these very files but had never come this close to finding something that was all but lost.

"But you already knew this, didn't you, Katarina?" Mr Stein asked. He held another photograph for them to see. "This is Renoir's *Two Boys Running Through a Field of Haystacks*." Kat and Hale leaned closer to the picture of two boys in a hayfield. One boy's hat had blown free and was tumbling through the meadow. They were chasing it.

"It was commissioned by a wealthy French official and pictures his two sons playing at his chateau near Nice. It hung in the oldest son's home in Paris until the German occupation. One of the brothers survived the camps. This" – Mr Stein stopped to wipe his eyes – "we had feared did not."

Kat and Hale sat quietly as Mr Stein told them about a Vermeer called *The Philosopher*, and a Rembrandt of the prodigal son. And, if possible, he grew even more serious as he held the final image towards them as carefully as if he were holding the missing masterpiece itself.

"Do you know this painting, Katarina?"

"No." Kat's voice cracked.

"*Look closely*," he urged again.

"I don't know it," Kat said, sensing his disappointment.

"It is called *Girl Praying to Saint Nicholas*," Mr Stein said, gazing at the picture again and then at Kat. "It is a long, long way from home."

Mr Stein studied Kat closely.

"Your mother used to sit in that very chair and listen to this old man rant about the lines on maps and laws in books that, even decades later, can stand between right and wrong. Countries with their laws of provenance," he scoffed. "Museums with fake bills of sale."

Mr Stein's sadness turned to fervour. "And that is why your mother came to this room… She told me that sometimes it takes a thief to catch a thief." His eyes shone. "You're going to steal these paintings, aren't you, Katarina?"

Kat wanted to explain everything, but right then the truth seemed like the cruellest thing of all.

"Mr Stein." Hale's voice was calm and even. "I'm

afraid it's a very long story."

The man nodded. "I see." He looked at Kat in the way of a man who had long since given up trying to right all the wrongs of the world himself.

"The men who took *Dancer Waiting in the Wings* from the Schulhoffs' dining room wall were evil, my dear. The men those men gave it to were evil. These paintings were traded for terrible favours in terrible times." Mr Stein took a deep breath. "No one good could have that group of paintings, Katarina." Kat nodded. "So wherever you have to go" – he stood – "whatever you have to do—"

He reached out his hand. And when Kat's small hand was wrapped in his own, he looked into her eyes and said, "Be careful."

Standing on Abiram Stein's front steps, facing the street, Kat felt very different from when she'd stood in that same spot forty minutes earlier, facing the door. Suspicions were facts. Fears were real. And ghosts were alive as she stood where her mother had once stood, unsure how to follow in her footsteps.

"It was good to see you again, Katarina," Mr Stein called from the doorway. "When I realized who you were…"

"Yes?" she asked, and Mr Stein smiled.

"I thought perhaps you were here because of what

happened at the Henley."

Hale was already at the car, but mention of the best museum in the world caught his attention. "What happened at the Henley?"

Mr Stein laughed a quick, throaty laugh. "You two should know better than I. It was *robbed*." He whispered that last word. "Or so they say," he added with a shrug, and despite everything, Kat managed to smile.

"Don't worry, Mr Stein. I'm afraid I've been in no position to rob the Henley."

"Oh." The older man nodded. "I know. The police, they are looking for someone already – a man named Visily Romani."

7 DAYS
UNTIL DEADLINE

LONDON,
ENGLAND

FIFTEEN

There are two dozen truly great museums in the world. Maybe two dozen and one if you don't mind the crowds at the Louvre, Kat's father always said. But, of course, even great museums are not created equal. Some are nothing but old houses with high ceilings and gorgeous mouldings, a few security cameras, and minimum-wage guards. Some hire consultants and get their equipment from the CIA.

And then there is the Henley.

"So this is the Henley," Hale said as they strolled through the great glass hall. His hands were in his pockets, and his hair was still damp from a shower. "It's smaller than I expected."

Kat had to stop. "You've never been to the Henley?"

He cocked his head. "Should alcoholics go to liquor stores?"

Kat kept walking.. "Point taken."

There were nine official entrances to the Henley, and

Kat was actually a little bit proud of herself for choosing the main doors (or any door, truth be told). Maybe she was maturing. Or maybe she was lazy. Or maybe she just loved the Henley foyer.

Two storeys of glass cut at dozens of angles framed the entrance. It was part solarium, part grand hall. Part sauna. The sun beat down, and despite the chilly wind that blew outside, the temperature inside the atrium was in the eighties at least. Men were taking off their suit coats. Women unwound scarves from around their necks. But Hale didn't break a sweat, and all Kat could do was look at him, and think *Cool*.

Two days before, the Henley had been closed until one in the afternoon, after a security guard doing his midnight rounds discovered a business card tucked between a painting and its frame. It was a small matter, really, except the guard had sworn that, at ten pm, no card had been there.

An alarm had been raised. More security officials had been called. And, unfortunately, so had a reporter from the local news. Scotland Yard had reviewed every piece of surveillance footage. Every member of the security staff, the cleaning crew, and the volunteer corps had been interviewed, but no one had seen anyone dangerously close to the painting in question.

And so, by Tuesday morning, the official stance of the official people, from the director of the Henley to the lead prosecutor at Scotland Yard, was that the guard was mistaken. The card must have been left by a guest earlier in the day and missed by housekeeping.

The unofficial stance of unofficial people was that someone from one of the old families was playing a joke. But Kat and Hale weren't laughing. And neither, Kat thought, was the Henley.

Standing in the long queue that day, Kat shifted on her feet. She crossed her arms. It felt as if her body held more energy – more nerves – than normal. She had to fight to keep them all in.

"I was here visiting the *Angel* exhibit in August," the woman in front of them told her companion. "There weren't metal detectors then."

Hale looked at Kat, and she read his mind. The metal detectors were new. If the metal detectors were new, what else was?

"Well, in August, mysterious men weren't breaking in and leaving their calling cards," the woman's companion replied.

They took a step forwards. "Maybe he was a handsome debonair thief who had a change of heart."

Kat blushed and thought about her father.

"Maybe he's here right now," the other woman said, giggling. "Scoping out the place?" She turned and scanned the atrium as if looking for the thief. What she saw was Hale, who nodded and smiled, and then it was the woman's turn to blush.

"I wouldn't mind meeting a dashing thief," the woman's friend whispered. Hale winked at Kat.

Kat raised her eyebrows and whispered, "I'd like to meet one of those, too."

Hale brought his hands to his chest, feigning injury, but Kat was far too worried and too tired to play along. She saw Hale looking at her and felt the hope that was growing inside of him. She pretended not to notice. "It's probably nothing," she told him.

He took a step. "Of course it is."

"I mean, in all likelihood, it's a coincidence," Kat said as if she really meant it.

"That's exactly what I was thinking," Hale lied.

The queue inched forwards. "We're probably wasting our time."

"I couldn't have said it better myself."

But the downside of being a con artist is that it makes you very hard to con. Even if the lies you tell are to yourself.

* * *

It was a most unusual day in what was shaping up to be the most unusual week in the Henley's anything-but-usual existence.

Even if Katarina Bishop didn't quite know to appreciate it, this fact was more than obvious to the guards, docents, custodians, staff, managers, and regular visitors who were all very well aware that queues never formed before nine am on weekdays. The elderly ladies in the burgundy blazers who sat at the information desk commented that the eight different school groups who were visiting that day all seemed particularly quiet, as if listening and looking for a ghost.

The floors in the Renaissance room always glowed a little brighter, and the frames hung a little straighter, and the painting at the centre of it – Leonardo da Vinci's *Angel Returning to Heaven* – always attracted more awestruck visitors than any other thing inside the Henley's walls. But on that morning, it felt very much as if the museum's crown jewel had somehow lost its shine.

Today, the Renaissance room stood empty as long queuesmoved down the marble halls, all heading for the exact same place.

"This is it."

Kat didn't have to read the sign on the entrance to know they'd reached the right collection. All she had to do was see the crowds and hear the whisper on the air: *Visily Romani*.

Tourists and scholars alike stood shoulder to shoulder, heel to toe, gawking, waiting to see the place where a card had mysteriously appeared in the middle of the night in one of the most secure buildings in all of London.

Kat and Hale didn't talk while they waited to enter the packed room. They didn't comment on the angles of the cameras or the positions of the guards. They were tourists too, in a way. Curious. Eager to know the truth about the very strange thing that had happened, but needing to know for entirely different reasons.

"He was here," Kat said when she finally made it inside. Most people looked for only a few seconds, then moved on. But Kat lingered. She and Hale were like the centre of a wheel, barely moving while the rest of the crowd circled past.

"Yeah, except he didn't *take* anything," Hale said.

"He was *there*." Kat felt her hand raise. She saw her finger point. Five paintings hung along the gallery's far wall. Two days before, Visily Romani had left his card tucked inside the frame of the centre painting.

A business card, the rumours said. White cardstock and black letters spelling out a name that, until then, had only been whispered in the darkest corners of the darkest rooms.

A calling card, left by a ghost, saying simply, *Visily Romani was here.*

Kat thought about that card, and something in her heart – or maybe just her blood – told her that of all the people who filled the Henley that day, the world's greatest thief was speaking directly to her.

"Why break in and not take anything?" Hale asked, but Kat shook her head.

She asked a better question: "Why break in and *leave* something?"

Kat stepped closer to the painting at the centre of it all. *Flowers on a Cool Spring Day*, it was called. It was a lovely little still life. The artist had been reasonably well-known. But there was nothing remarkable about it besides the fact that this was the place where Visily Romani had chosen to leave his card.

Kat stayed back, staring at the other five paintings in the room, trying to guess what Romani had been thinking.

She closed her eyes and remembered the stories she'd heard her whole life – legends of the greatest thief who never lived:

A man walked into the Kremlin and walked out with a Fabergé egg under his top hat.

A corrupt German art dealer sold a fake Rembrandt to an Englishman, not aware that stolen Nazi plans were hidden inside.

Now five paintings were missing.

Kat stared at the gallery wall.

Five paintings remained.

She made a slow rotation, scrutinizing each of the paintings, studying their dimensions. She felt her heart start to race.

"What if that card wasn't all he left?"

"What?" Hale asked, turning to look at her, but Kat was already walking forwards, examining the ornate frames around the priceless works.

"Miss," one of the docents said as Kat leaned forward. "Miss, I'm afraid I'm going to have to ask you to step back." The man eased between Kat and the painting, but not before the idea had already taken root in Hale's mind.

"No," Hale started, and then he looked from the paintings and back to Kat again. "Why would someone break into the Henley to *leave* five priceless paintings..." He looked at the walls. Counted. "*Behind* five different paintings?" He didn't even try to hide the awe in his voice.

Because he's done things like this before, Kat wanted to say. Because using the name Romani means you always have a plan – a reason. Because Psuedonima jobs aren't ordinary jobs. Because Visily Romani isn't an ordinary thief.

"But why would someone do that?"

"I don't know, Hale."

"But why would—"

"I…I don't know."

She suddenly felt the need to be free of the crowds and the noise and the history that hung on every wall, taunting her.

"Somebody's playing games!" Kat said angrily as she left the exhibit hall and started down the Henley's grand promenade. She walked faster, Hale beside her, trying to keep up. "Somebody's having fun! And he doesn't care that other people are going to get hurt because of it."

People were starting to stare, so Hale placed his arm around her shoulder and tried to stop her – to calm her.

"I know," he whispered. "But maybe it's a good thing."

"Maybe it's what? Taccone's after my dad, Hale. Taccone—"

"Maybe it means we've found them. And if they can be found…"

It seemed to Katarina Bishop as if all the moments in her family's very long, very dubious past had been preparing her to say, "They can be stolen."

SIXTEEN

As Kat watched the city roll by from the back of a long black car, she was acutely aware of the fact that she had three – maybe four – options.

Option one: she could call Arturo Taccone and tell him to meet her at the Henley. How he got the paintings off the wall and out the door was his problem. This, of course, was the option that made the most sense, incurred the least amount of risk, and, given what Mr Stein had told them, was most likely to get her thrown into Arturo Taccone's moat. Therefore, it was an option she didn't consider for long.

If they had been any other kind of paintings – or if Arturo Taccone had been any other kind of man – then option number two would have been the clear winner. All it required was a five minute phone call to the Henley's director and the suggestion that a business card might not have been all Visily Romani left behind. But there was no way Kat could be certain that Taccone's hold over the paintings was legal enough to see them returned, or illegal enough to see him arrested. The only thing Kat knew for certain was that if she caused Taccone to lose the things he loved, then eventually, he would return the favour.

The third option was still forming vaguely in the back of her mind, but she knew it would almost certainly involve a lecture from her father and a general call to arms of every lock man, pyro geek, wheeler, and/or inside player in the business. Given recent events, it would probably also involve a lot of Kat being looked at and talked to like someone's daughter and niece. It would most certainly include the very real risk that Arturo Taccone's paintings would not be the only ones liberated from the Henley collection. That is, if Uncle Eddie said so.

But Uncle Eddie had said it was over. Uncle Eddie had said it was sacred, and if he didn't think Kat could (or should) undo what Visily Romani had done, then there was no thief in the world who would attempt it. Still, Kat's mind kept coming back to option three.

Maybe because that was the best of the options. Or maybe, she feared, because it was the option that was in her blood.

"We don't have a lot of time," Hale was saying. "For a target the size of the Henley, we'll have to—"

"This is nuts." Kat blurted more for her own benefit than for Hale's. "Stealing from this Visily Romani guy – whoever he is – that's one thing. But stealing" – she stopped, glanced at the back of Marcus's head, and lowered her voice – "from *THE HENLEY*?"

When the car stopped, Kat and Hale got out. Kat walked quickly, crunching gravel beneath her feet, and ran her hand through her hair – the very gesture she'd seen her father make a thousand times…

Right before he agreed to do something stupid.

"I mean, even if we did," she said, glancing up at Hale as he kept pace beside her, "it's *the Henley*."

"Yeah," Hale said, his voice cool.

"No one has ever stolen a painting from the Henley."

"Yeah," Hale said again, his excitement rising.

Kat stopped. "We'd be stealing *five*."

"Well, technically, we'd be *re*-stealing them," he said dryly. "It's kind of like a double negative."

She turned from him again and started across a wide stretch of grass, going nowhere in particular. Just going. "Assuming we could do it, it'd take a big crew."

"Yeah, and no one really likes you," Hale added. He didn't smile.

The wind was cold beneath the grey sky. Leaves blew across the ground at their feet. "We'd need gear – the good stuff. The really expensive stuff."

"Too bad I'm only good for my looks," Hale said. "And my better-than-average singing voice."

Kat rolled her eyes. *"Seven days, Hale."*

This time he had no response, no solution. If there was one thing Kat learned from losing her mother, it was that even the best thief in the world can't steal time.

Kat looked over the rolling hills, the stone fences that crisscrossed the horizon. London felt a million miles away. "Where are we?"

Hale pointed behind her. "Country house," he said, but of course, by *house*, he meant *mansion*.

Kat turned to see a perfectly planned garden spread out along one side of a massive estate. Smoke spiralled from at least three chimneys. She imagined that somewhere in that grand old building, Marcus would soon be preparing soup and tea.

She missed Uncle Eddie.

They started for the great stone house, the weight of what they had to do settling down on them.

"Mr Stein—" Kat started, but Hale cut her off.

"Don't think about it."

"They aren't Taccone's paintings, Hale."

He stopped her. Her arms felt especially small in his hands as he held her there, staring into her eyes. "First, we save your dad, Kat." There was an urgency in his voice that made Kat forget to fight as Hale narrowed her options down to one. "First, we rob the Henley."

He put his arm around her and led her towards the house where W. W. Hale the First had been born.

"We're gonna need people," Kat said as Marcus opened the big double doors. "People we can trust," she added.

Hale nodded and walked her down the ornate hall, pausing before a pair of sliding doors. He pushed them aside, revealing a two-storey library, a warm fire, and the familiar faces of the Bagshaw brothers, Simon, and Gabrielle.

"You mean, like them?"

SEVENTEEN

The assembly of a crew is a monumental event in a young thief's life. There are meetings and phone calls. Plans, and occasionally, a celebratory cake. Normal families have graduations. Thief families have this. Kat should have felt a little cheated that she'd missed out on all the fun. But she didn't.

She looked at Hale. He shrugged. "I had a hunch." And then he helped himself to one of the finger sandwiches that Marcus was circulating around the room, popping it whole into his mouth, barely taking time to chew before reaching for the tray again.

No one shook hands or said hello. Kat's friends looked as if they were prepared to stay all night, planning. And even though they were essentially in a circle, Kat saw the way they watched her, and for the first time in her life, she knew what it felt like to be at the head of the table.

"Thanks for coming." She took a step closer, gripped

the back of a Queen Anne chair. "I've got sort of a job."

"I knew it!" Hamish exclaimed. "I told Angus when we saw you at Uncle Eddie's that something was happening – didn't I? So what is it?" He rubbed his hands together. "Jewellery shop?"

"Maybe a bank job?" Angus guessed.

Hamish nodded. "You know I do adore a proper bank heist. They're so preferable to…improper ones."

"It's not a job like anyone here has ever done before," Hale said, giving the Bagshaws a look that said quite clearly there would be no need for anyone to interrupt Kat again.

In that moment, the room seemed to find a new energy. Simon's fingers twitched. The brothers leaned closer. Even Gabrielle seemed to be giving her cousin her full attention as Kat searched their eyes and drew a breath.

"Whatever we do next," she blurted, "we do *without* Uncle Eddie's blessing."

No one responded at first. Then Hamish looked at his big brother, smiling, as if waiting for permission to laugh. It had to be a joke, after all. But Gabrielle was stoic, and Simon was mumbling about Vegas, and growing pale. And, most of all, *something* had pulled Kat back into their world.

Hale dimmed the lights and turned on the television. The same black-and-white video that had been haunting

Kat's dreams started to play.

"This is a private villa in Italy." The frame froze on the empty gallery-style room. "And I mean *private*."

"How do we get in?" Angus asked, inching closer to the screen.

Hale and Kat looked at each other. She shook her head. "We don't."

Then, as if on cue, the man they called Romani came onto the screen. "Someone has already done us that favour."

They watched the artist work for a few moments.

"Hey, Kat," Simon started, "is that—"

"It's *not* my dad!"

"I was gonna say, is that a Degas?"

"Oh, yes," she said slowly. She thought of Mr Stein. "There were five paintings in all. Old Masters."

"Who is this bloke?" Hamish asked.

"Does it matter?" Hale asked. Hamish shrugged, but every eye in the room was on Kat.

This was the time, of course, to tell them the whole story. It was also the time to lie. Kat asked herself what her father would do — what Uncle Eddie might say.

So Kat settled on the lie she knew was truest: "That guy is Visily Romani."

Kat wasn't surprised to hear their silence.

Simon was the only one who moved. "The Visily

Romani who robbed five Swiss banks in one night in 1932? The Visily Romani who made off with half the crown jewels of Russia in 1960?" Sweat gathered on Simon's brow. "*The* Visily Romani?"

Hale leaned back and crossed his legs. "Don't worry, Simon." He popped another sandwich into his mouth. "It's way worse than you think."

Kat could practically feel the Bagshaws' excitement. Hamish rubbed his hands across the tops of his thighs, warming them, getting ready for something – anything.

Angus seemed to be calculating something in his head. "If he did a job in thirty-two, doesn't that make him kind of...old?"

"Visily Romani is one of the Pseudonimas – the sacred names," Kat explained.

"So this guy..." Angus trailed off, but pointed to the man on the screen.

"He could be anyone," Simon finished.

Kat turned and stared out the window at the gardens and the grounds, the trappings of Hale's world, as she thought about the laws of hers. "He could be anywhere."

Simon was rising and starting to pace. "So we're all here because we've got to..." he stammered, pointing to the screen. "You mean this is a..." He stopped and put his hands on his hips. His shirt was peeking out from underneath his sweater vest. His face was growing redder by the second. "I was under the impression that Pseudonimas are slightly..."

"Not to be messed with?" Gabrielle answered for him. Then she smiled. "Oh, they're not. Or, well, they weren't."

"You can walk away right now. All of you," Kat reminded them. "Uncle Eddie has already said it can't – or maybe that it *shouldn't* – be done." She drew a deep breath, wondering for a moment if there was a difference. "I won't blame any of you if you turn and leave right—"

"You kidding?" Hamish asked. "There's a few hundred million Euros on those walls. Easy." He glanced at his brother. "We're in."

"Yeah," Kat said slowly. "Well, like I said, it's not a *typical* job." Kat didn't know what was harder – what she had to say, or the way everyone looked at her while she said it. "Mr Taccone has" – Kat considered her words carefully – "asked for our assistance retrieving the paintings."

"So...what? There's some kind of finder's fee?" Angus asked.

"It's not quite like that," Kat admitted.

"More like a promise that Taccone won't drown Uncle Bobby in his moat," Gabrielle said simply.

Kat gave a weak smile as she looked at everyone. "And I'll owe you."

Kat expected her friends to need a moment to think. They should have taken a walk around the grounds to clear their heads, put their thoughts in order. Kat expected half of them to do her family proud and slip away noiselessly into the night, but amazingly, that didn't happen.

Instead, Hamish slapped his brother on the back and said, "We're in. Whatever you need, Kat."

Simon held his hand to his mouth, biting his nails as he stared into space. Calculating. "Is Uncle Eddie going to find out about this?"

"Come on, Simon," Hale answered. "What are the odds he already knows?"

The Bagshaws looked at each other, spoke at the exact same time. "Two to one."

Simon gulped. But eventually he said, "OK."

Kat looked at Gabrielle, who had started polishing her toenails. The girl didn't even look up, but as Kat opened her mouth to speak, Gabrielle said, "Duh," and Kat knew there was nothing else to say on the subject.

"Great. Thanks. I guess we'll start casing the target tomorrow."

"What *is* the target?" Angus said slowly.

Hale looked at Kat. For a moment it seemed OK.

And then Kat said, "The Henley."

6 DAYS
UNTIL DEADLINE

LONDON,
ENGLAND

EIGHTEEN

If you lived in 1921, and if you had more money than time, and if you were a woman, then there were very few acceptable ways in which you were allowed to fill your days. Some played cards. Others played music. Most surrounded themselves with dresses and hats, perfectly tended gardens and expertly steeped cups of tea. But Veronica Miles Henley had not belonged in 1921...not really. And so Veronica Henley had turned her great fortune to her great passion and almost single-handedly built the greatest museum in the world.

Or so Katarina Bishop's mother had told her. And so Kat herself still believed.

"Better than the Louvre?" Hale's voice cut through the sound of the fountain in front of the glass-covered main entrance.

Kat rolled her eyes. "Too crowded."

"The Tate?"

"Too pretentious."

"The Egyptian Museum in Cairo?"

Kat leaned back and let her fingers trail through the water. "Way too hot."

The surveillance cameras mounted on the walls that circled the Henley saw all of this, of course. They were perfectly positioned and highly calibrated – the best they could possibly be.

The two guards who stood sentry by each gate no doubt noticed the boy and girl who lingered by the fountain, eating sandwiches, throwing crumbs to the birds that landed on the square – just like a thousand other teenage couples that gathered here each year.

The guards might have seen the boy throw his arm around the girl's neck and hold a camera out in front of them, snapping pictures. They might have noticed how the couple paced from one end of the wall to the next. They didn't, of course, see that the pictures were really of the positions of the cameras; that their paced steps were mapping out the dimensions of the perimeter wall.

They were simply two teens who appeared to be in the midst of a great autumn.

But, of course, the guards didn't see a lot of things.

* * *

If the guards at the Henley didn't pay much attention to the boy and girl who were lingering outside, they certainly didn't notice the two brothers who stood in line by the café, messing around, taking silly pictures of things like doors and vents as they waited for a table. They did not see the pale boy with the backpack and a small digital gaming device who wandered the halls aimlessly...until he actually ran into one of the docents on patrol, falling to the hard floor in the process.

The device in his hand skidded across the marble floor.

"No!" the boy cried, chasing it. But as soon as it skidded to a stop at the feet of one of the Henley guards, the boy froze.

The guard leaned down and picked up the device. If he'd been more focused on the boy than the toy, he might have noticed that Simon was holding his breath and was every bit as pale as the marble statue that stood behind him. But the guard was too captivated by the maze of grids and dots and lines that filled the screen to notice the boy. "What is this?"

"Nothing!" Simon blurted far too quickly, but his baby face was too innocent to cause any worry for the docent and the guard.

The docent looked over the guard's shoulder. "That's Underworld Warrior Two, isn't it?" the docent asked, leaning closer to examine the screen.

"Hey, what's this—" The guard started hitting the red button, and Simon winced.

"Don't… Don't… Please don't…"

"It's really different from Underworld Warrior One, huh?" the guard asked, still punching the button, not knowing the chaos he was causing in the guardroom twenty feet away as every motion sensor in the building began to flash. "What's this do?" The guard moved to a different button, but before he could short-circuit every electrical device within a dozen yards, Simon lunged for him.

"It's sort of a…prototype," he said, snatching the device out of the guard's hand before the man's colleagues noticed that anything was wrong. It should be pointed out that this was in fact the truth, and so Simon had no trouble saying, "My dad designs these things."

The guard eyed the device again, then patted Simon on the back. "Lucky you. Watch where you're going, OK?"

"Will do," Simon said, and that, more than anything, wasn't a lie.

The docents at the Henley were used to seeing almost every sort of behaviour from the thousands of guests who paraded through the museum each year.

But when a teenage girl in amazingly high heels

stumbled through the halls that day, there was something about her that simply demanded the guards' attention. Some said later it was her short skirt. Others wisely observed that it was more likely the legs that protruded beneath it. Whatever the case, their eyes were most certainly not on her hands.

"Wow!" the girl exclaimed too loudly as she walked into the room that had recently become known as the Romani Room. She craned her head to look at the ornate ceiling overhead. "That's tall!"

The docents at the Henley did not know what every thief knows – that if there's no way to do something without being seen, then it's best to do it in a way that will be well and fully stared at.

"That," Gabrielle said, spinning on her high heels and pointing at the painting that hung at the centre of the room, "is pretty!"

The guards who were monitoring the Romani Room that day had never been accused of being lazy or slow, of being dense or unaware. But that did not change the fact that they had never seen a seemingly intoxicated young woman teeter across a marble floor and lunge for a painting worth a quarter of a million dollars.

The tourists, who, so far, had been far too proper to openly stare, had to hurry out of the way. The guards, who had been too busy studying the young woman's legs to notice where those legs were carrying her, could only gape.

Her hand brushed against the frame, and her legs immediately stopped being the most interesting thing about her.

A shock echoed throughout the room. Metal grates descended from the ceiling, blocking the doors in a split second while women screamed and children cried and a siren pierced the air so loudly that men dropped their children's hands to cover their own ears.

Even the guards cringed and bent over, the crackles of their walkie-talkies lost in the chaos of sirens and trapped tourists. When they remembered the girl with the long legs and the short skirt who lay on the cold marble floor, she was too unconscious and too pretty for anyone at the Henley to stay angry for long.

No one noticed the way Kat stood on the other side of the grates watching everything unfold, plugs in her ears blocking out the sound. Plans were already taking shape in her mind as she turned and walked slowly towards the exit.

If it hadn't been for the alarms and the grates, the trapped tourists and the unconscious girl, someone at the Henley might have noticed the two thugs who appeared at Kat's side as if from nowhere.

They might have seen Kat and the men disappear behind the tinted glass of a stretch limousine and noted that Kat didn't scream.

They might have heard her say, "Hello, Signor Taccone."

NINETEEN

The first thing Kat did, of course, was kick herself. She should have been expecting this. She should have heard them coming. But the alarms had been too loud and the earplugs too effective, and her mind had been too distracted by the serious work she had to do, and so Kat's guard was down that day. But she wasn't going to let Arturo Taccone know it.

He smiled frostily at her from the other side of the limo's backseat, and despite everything, she was almost glad for the warmth of the thuglike bodies on either side of her.

"Your efforts are entertaining, Katarina," he said with a slight laugh. "Ineffective, but entertaining."

Kat thought back to the sight of her cousin slumping to the cold floor of the gallery while the Henley's state-of-the-art defences were put to the test by a sixteen-year-old girl. And her legs.

"I told you I wasn't the right person for the job," Kat

said. "Now, there's a Japanese crew that comes highly recommended. I could get you a name and number if you're interested."

Taccone's dismissive wave made Kat realize that he was enjoying this. She thought of his hidden bunker, and she knew somehow that the joy he got from keeping things so beautiful and precious under lock and key was nothing compared to the thrill of following them across Europe. Paintings are just things, after all. What Arturo Taccone really loved was the chase.

"So tell me, Katarina" – he jerked his head in the direction of the grand old building that was disappearing in the distance – "what are you going to steal? Da Vinci's *Angel*, perhaps? I would pay handsomely to add that to my collection, you know."

"I'm not a thief," Kat said. He looked at her. "*Anymore*," she added. "I'm not a thief anymore."

Taccone didn't try to hide the amusement in his eyes. "And yet here you are."

"I'm here to get *your* paintings, Signor Taccone, so technically I'm re-stealing." Again, Hale's voice echoed in her head. "Re-stealing is more like a double negative."

"You think your father has hidden my paintings inside the Henley?" Taccone scoffed, a cruel guttural sound. "And exactly why would he do that?"

"Not my dad," she said. "Remember?"

"Oh, Katarina," he said with a sigh. "If not your father, then who?"

She thought for a moment about Visily Romani – about a legend, a ghost. But he wasn't a ghost, not really. Somewhere in the world there was a man – a very real man – with blood and bones and the necessary knowledge to break into the most secure museum in the world, and to use that particular name to do it.

So somewhere, yes, there was a man. And his name was *not* Visily Romani. But somehow Kat doubted that Arturo Taccone would understand.

"I did find them, Signor Taccone," Kat said, moving closer, sitting up. "I can tell you where they are, and then I guess you won't need me anymore. After all" – she gestured behind them – "as you saw, my friends and I are not really suited for an opportunity of this magnitude."

"Ah, but Katarina, I think you're suited quite nicely."

He smiled at her, and Kat couldn't help herself: a part of her wondered whether this man had more faith in her than her own uncle, maybe even more than her own father. But then again, this man didn't care if she ended up dead or in prison as long as he got his paintings back, so maybe he wasn't the best judge of her abilities.

"We need more time." It was a statement, not a plea,

and Kat was surprised by how steady her voice stayed as she said it. "This is the Henley. No one has *ever* robbed the Henley."

"If you're correct, then your father got through their security to place my paintings—"

"Look!" Kat didn't know she was reaching for him until she felt his walking stick in her hands. "You don't believe me when I say my dad didn't steal your paintings, fine. You don't believe me when I say they're in that building, OK. But they are. And believe me when I say no crew is going to take on the Henley in six days. It's not going to happen. It can't be done."

Kat felt the thugs on either side of her shifting. She knew that in the game Arturo Taccone was playing, she had just changed the rules, and that the thugs, for all their might and muscle, had never considered that anyone would ever touch their boss – much less a shorter-than-average fifteen-year-old girl.

"Did you know they've got at least a hundred guards working three eight-hour overlapping shifts?" Kat asked. "And they're not cheap rent-a-cops either. Most are former law enforcement. All are well trained, and there's a five-week waiting period for background checks before they hire any new people, so there's no getting anyone on the inside."

She felt her momentum building, and Taccone let her talk.

"Did you know they've got the same kind of surveillance cameras the CIA uses on their annexe buildings at Langley? And that's not even counting the pressure-sensitive floor panels or the electrified frames that my dear cousin was kind enough to point out. And did I mention the pressure switches? Of course, I don't know anything about them...*because it's the Henley*...and they don't exactly post their security specs on the Internet, but you can bet your friends' weight in gold that they've got sensors on the backs of those paintings so sensitive that if a fly landed on one, the whole place would lock down before you could say 'Renaissance'."

He smiled again, slower this time, and it sent a chill through Kat as sharp as any winter wind.

"I'm going to miss our little chats, Katarina. You should know that it's out of respect for your mother's family that I have tried to do this in the most honourable way possible. I've told you what I want. I've given you more than enough time to comply. And yet no one has returned my paintings." He sounded genuinely surprised – as if he'd been waiting every day for them to come in the post.

Kat leaned closer, and now there was no disguising the fear in her voice. "I. Can't. Do it."

"Don't worry, Katarina. Six days from now, if I still don't have my paintings, I'll simply pay your father a visit and ask him myself."

"He doesn't know," Kat shot back, but Taccone continued.

"Perhaps, by that time, his friends from Interpol will be gone and then I can speak to him myself. Yes" – he nodded slowly – "when the time comes, your father will get me what I need."

Kat started to speak, but before she could say a word, Taccone turned to thug 1. "Aren't you hot in those gloves?"

But it wasn't hot – not at all. Kat held her breath as the large man pulled the glove from his left hand and rested it on his left knee, inches from the walking stick that she was holding. When Kat had first seen the stick's pewter handle, she had thought the ornate pattern was pretty. But that was before she saw the identical pattern on the hand beside her, a scar – a warning – seared forever into flesh.

"When the time comes, I'll simply ask your father." Taccone's voice was cold and cruel. "Don't worry, Katarina. I can be quite persuasive."

The car slowed. Kat felt something land in her lap, and glanced down to see a large manila envelope.

"In the meantime, Katarina, I do wish you luck in your

endeavours." Again, he didn't mock. He truly seemed to believe in her as he took back his walking stick and said, "You have *so many* reasons to succeed."

Thug 1 opened the door and stepped from the car. With his scarred hand, he gestured for her to follow.

Kat stood perfectly still for a long time on the pavement of Trafalgar Square – the envelope too heavy in her hands. She held her breath and looked inside. Photographs. But not just photographs. There was a very different word that came to Katarina Bishop's mind: *Leverage*.

She felt sick. The cold wind froze her to the bone. Red double-decker buses and bright neon lights surrounded her, reflecting off the black-and-white images in her hands. Of all the pictures in Arturo Taccone's life, probably few had brought him as much enjoyment as the ones she held now.

Gabrielle boarding a train in Vienna, her hair blowing in the wind.

Hale striding through the lobby of a Las Vegas hotel.

Her father sipping coffee, crossing a crowded Paris square.

Uncle Eddie sitting on a park bench in Brooklyn.

The people she most cared about were depicted there in black-and-white and the message was clear: Arturo Taccone knew how to find the people and things that were important to her, and if Kat didn't do the same, he wouldn't be the only one to lose something he loved.

For the first time in Katarina Bishop's life, she truly understood that a picture is worth a thousand words.

TWENTY

Kat was late coming home. To the Hale family's country home, that is. Kat's only home was a brownstone in New York, and the man who ruled that household had strictly forbidden her from doing what she was doing.

She felt the envelope of photographs rub against her bare stomach, where she'd tucked it beneath the waistband of her jeans. Hiding it. The foyer was big and cold and empty. Paintings of Hales long since dead and gone lined the hall. Kat imagined them keeping watch, waiting for some living breathing member of the family to come home.

Kat missed Uncle Eddie.

She suddenly craved soup.

She wanted to talk to her father.

She took a step and felt the envelope against her stomach again, and instantly, she wanted to call everyone she ever knew and tell them to scatter – to hide. But the only people she knew were professional thieves. They never stopped hiding.

"*Angus, she's back!*" Hamish Bagshaw's voice had changed, Kat was sure of it. He sat at the bottom of the stairs, waiting for her along the way.

As he chomped his gum and grinned, his brother stepped into the hallway, carrying a bowl of ice. "Brilliant," Angus said.

Kat wanted to keep walking, but Angus stepped in front of her.

"We were hoping we might have a minute of your valuable time," he said.

Hamish cast a quick glance down the empty hall and then added, "Alone."

Angus was eleven months older than his brother, and slightly taller. They both had hair that was somewhere between red and blond, and skin that looked as if it might burn even on a cloudy day. Their shoulders were broad but their arms were scrawny, and Kat realized that they were still growing – that they were still a long way from being men.

"What is it?" Kat asked.

"We've been meaning to talk to you for a while about… well…recent unfortunate events, and we just wanted to say—"

"Wait." Kat stopped him. "What *recent unfortunate events*?"

"Well…" Hamish started. "We had a bit of trouble on a job a while back."

"In Luxembourg?" Kat asked.

"Did ol' Hale tell you about that, then?" Hamish asked. "That was a right good con, that was—"

"Hamish!" Kat snapped. The brothers shook their heads.

"*After* Luxembourg," Angus clarified.

"What—" Kat started, but Hamish was already throwing his arm around her, saying, "You know what I love about you, Kat?"

"Besides your beauty," Angus interjected, even though, to Kat's knowledge, neither of them had ever noticed she was female.

"Besides that," Hamish confirmed with a nod.

"And your mind," Angus added.

"A truly great mind," Hamish agreed.

"Guys." Kat felt her patience wane. "*What happened?*"

"You see, Kat, it wasn't so much *what*…" Angus let the word linger.

"As *who*," his brother finished.

Angus pulled away, then studied her. "You really haven't heard?" As Kat shook her head, his gaze fell to the floor. "Wow, Kat, you really were gone, weren't you?"

More than the feeling of walking back into Uncle Eddie's kitchen, the look on the two brothers' faces told her that it was true – she had done it. Katarina Bishop had really left the life. Once. For a little while. It hadn't been a dream.

"What happened?" Kat asked.

"It's not that bad, really," Hamish said. "We shouldn't have—"

"Am I going to have to call Uncle Eddie?" she threatened.

"We didn't know they were nuns!"

There is a rule older than the Chelovek Pseudonima – a truth not even the greatest liar can deny: You cannot con an honest man. But if you do…

You'll regret it.

"We're blacklisted, Kat," Angus admitted with a guilty glance at his brother. "Uncle Eddie says we can't work for a while, but your dad's always been good to us, so if you say leave, we leave. If you say we're in…"

Kat stood there looking at the very boys who had stolen the first tooth she had ever lost and tried to ransom it to the tooth fairy; the two young men who had once stolen a Tyrannosaurus rex from the Museum of Natural History – one bone at a time.

"Guys, Uncle Eddie doesn't want *anyone* doing this job." Kat turned and started through the big sprawling house, calling behind her, "You're in!"

Walking into the library a moment later, Kat knew something was wrong.

For starters, Simon was even paler than usual. Gabrielle lay on the sofa, her feet propped up, a damp rag on her forehead; her hair was significantly frizzier, and as Angus placed the bowl of ice beside her, neither Bagshaw even tried to look down her shirt.

"Welcome back." She noticed Hale leaning against a window seat on the far side of the room, not quite sitting and not quite standing. He pushed away from the wall. "So glad you could join us."

Kat felt the envelope slide against her stomach. She could have sworn she heard it scrape against the denim, as loud as a scream in the quiet room. But it was her ears playing tricks on her. Her mind. Maybe her cool was one more thing she'd lost at Colgan.

"Oh, I'm *fine*, Kat," Gabrielle replied to the unasked question with a dramatic wave of her good hand. "I'm sure the burns on my feet are going to heal in no time."

But no one else said anything. They all just looked at Kat, none of them wanting to be the bearer of bad news.

"What?" Kat asked, looking around the room.

"Simon," Hale said, dropping onto one of the leather sofas and propping his feet up. He gestured for the boy to begin.

"The paramedics were quite sure the dizziness would subside eventually," Gabrielle offered from the couch. Everyone ignored her.

"Well," Simon said slowly. Three different laptops were spread out before him. The small device he'd carried through the Henley was plugged into one, and a three-dimensional schematic flashed across the screens. "It's" – Simon looked as if he were trying to recall the right technical term – "complicated."

"They gave me this wonderful ointment for the scalded tips of my fingers," Gabrielle added. No one heard.

"Do you want the bad news or the good news?" Simon asked.

"Good," Kat and Hale said at the same time.

"The Henley has spent the last six months updating all of its security features – which were already good. I mean *Henley good* – so the new stuff is—"

"I thought you said this was the good news," Hale said.

Simon nodded. "A change like this doesn't happen overnight, so they're doing it exhibit by exhibit, starting with the most valuable rooms, and…"

"The Romani Room isn't the top of the list?" Kat guessed.

Simon shook his head. "Not even close. So if the Henley is vulnerable anywhere, this is it."

Kat had spent hours wondering why *that* room of that museum. She knew it hadn't been random. There was a reason a thief like Romani would pick that exhibit over the Renaissance room or any of the Henley's other crown jewels, and this was it. She smiled. Somehow the world was starting to make sense again.

"And the bad news?" Hale asked.

Simon shrugged. "It's still the Henley."

It took a moment for the words to sink in – for everyone to realize the magnitude of what had to be done. Success in Kat's world depended so much on details that the big pictures were frequently lost. But Kat knew what they were doing. And as the moment stretched out, everyone else seemed to remember too.

"It's totally a closed-circuit feed," Simon went on, a moment later. "There's no way we're hacking in from the outside. But we knew that already."

"Why don't you skip to the parts we *don't* know?" Hale said impatiently.

"Right," Simon said, pointing at Hale as if that were a brilliant idea. "They've already updated all the wiring in the whole building. Really state-of-the-art stuff. I mean, it's awesome—"

"Simon," Hale snapped.

"Well…that's the bad news," Simon finished. "There's no hacking it. Even if I could tie into the mainframe, I couldn't override their system."

"I'm really hoping there's good news," Hamish added.

Simon smiled. "Remodelling old buildings like the Henley is…awkward," he said, his eyes shining.

"And…" Hale prompted.

"And so sometimes when they put new systems in…" Simon started, but Kat was already nodding.

"They leave the old systems right where they are," she finished. She looked at Hale, and together they said, "Like the Dubai job."

Simon nodded. "I'm not saying I can get it up and running, but if I can get into a high-security room for fifteen minutes, and if I'm right…that's our way into the Henley's inner sanctums."

"Do it," Hale said, then stopped. He looked at Kat and waved, an *after you* gesture.

Kat turned to her cousin. "So, Gabrielle, what did we learn?"

Gabrielle glared at her. "We learned that the next time you want to find out what kind of frontline defence mechanisms someone has in place, you can..." but she trailed off as she fell back on the pillow. "What was I saying?"

Kat looked at the brothers.

"Exhibit hall grates fell one point two seconds after contact," Angus told her.

"The main hall was locked down less than five seconds after that," Hamish added, crossing his leg. "We won't be doing anything that requires a hasty break for the nearest exit, I can tell you that."

"Yeah," Angus agreed. "Those Henley guards didn't look like the sort who would let us walk out the front door with five paintings under our arms in the middle of the day."

"Even if they aren't *their* paintings," his brother said.

"Great," Gabrielle said from the sofa. "I ruined my nails for nothing."

"Not for nothing," Kat said. "Thanks to you, Gabs, we just figured out half a dozen ways *not* to rob the Henley."

"Mary Poppins?" Hale suggested four hours later.

"Do *you* know a way to make it rain between now and Tuesday?" Gabrielle replied.

"Five O'Clock Shadows?" Hamish asked.

"Backup generators only give us fifteen seconds," Simon said with a shake of his head.

They'd been through every con they'd ever heard of, and a few Kat guessed the Bagshaw brothers had made up on the spot, but she didn't notice the time until she saw Gabrielle stifle a yawn. Kat was too consumed by a ticking clock in the back of her mind. A deadline. A plan. She stared at the lists and diagrams they'd drawn in Magic Marker, and after that had dried up, eyeliner, all over the glass of the library windows.

"It's no use," Hale said, dropping to one of the leather sofas. "If we had a month…maybe."

"We don't," Kat told him.

"If we had two maybe three more people…"

Kat closed her eyes. "We don't."

"Princess Bride?" Hamish offered, but his brother turned to him.

"Do you know where we can find a six-fingered man on such short notice?"

Kat could feel the air changing – the hope slipping away. Maybe they were too tired. Maybe they'd simply been closed up in that room for too long. But she actually jumped when she heard Hale say, "We need to call Uncle Eddie."

"No." Kat had *thought* it, of course. But it took her

a moment to realize the voice that answered belonged to Gabrielle. "Uncle Eddie said no. Don't you guys get it? If he said no, then…" she trailed off. It seemed to take all of her energy to sit upright on the sofa.

"*We* have to do it," Kat finished.

Simon looked at Kat. "What about at night? Romani did it at night."

If Romani did it, Kat thought but didn't dare say. She didn't want to remind anyone – least of all herself – that there might be nothing behind those five paintings but the most sensitive antitheft devices ever designed by man. That this might be, in every way, a ghost hunt, a fool's errand. The greatest con the greatest con man to never live had ever pulled.

"You see these, Kat?" Hale gestured to the plan-covered windows. "One of these plans might work – *maybe* – for the best eight-man crew in the world. Except" – he turned, doing a quick headcount – "yeah, there are still just six of us."

"We can do it with six."

"Six makes it risky."

"Yeah," Kat said, spinning on him. "So was serving as the grease man when Dad robbed the Tower of London when I was five, but I did it."

In the corner, Hamish and Angus were smiling.

"Good times," Angus said.

"You were late tonight." Hale's voice was cool, even cold, and Kat knew this was the time to tell him about the photos. Either that or walk away.

"Gabrielle—" she turned and looked at her cousin – "thanks. And um…moisturize. Simon," Kat said as she tried not to look at Hale, "while I'm gone, figure out how to get eyes and ears in there."

"Sure," Simon said. "We could run a… Wait. Where are you going?"

When Kat reached the doorway, somehow Marcus was already there, a suitcase in his hand. "I believe you'll be needing this, miss"

Hale sighed. "Paris?" He looked away. "Say hi to your dad."

5 DAYS
UNTIL DEADLINE

PARIS,
FRANCE

TWENTY-ONE

Amelia Bennett had not been the youngest person in Interpol's Art Crime division to achieve the rank of detective. She was not the only woman. And yet, in an agency that was in every way a part of the Old Boy network, it was impossible for anyone to look at her without first registering that she was neither old nor boy. This was only part of the mystery that surrounded her when she'd moved from London to the Paris branch. The thing that *most* mystified the professional mystery solvers of the small branch of Interpol's main European office was that Amelia Bennett was so lucky.

And this morning, of course, was no exception.

No sooner had she walked into the cramped, unglamourous office, than one of her Old Boy colleagues met her at the door.

"You've got a witness to your gallery robbery," he said in English, and Detective Bennett did not seem the least bit surprised that her cold case was warm again. "An American girl," the man continued. "A tourist. She was down the street the night of the break-in. She says she saw a man in the area, acting suspiciously."

At this, Detective Bennett raised her eyebrows. "Is he anyone we know?"

The man smiled and led her into the room where the young girl sat waiting.

"Thank you so much for coming in. I'm Detective Bennett," the woman said. "I'm sorry. I don't believe I got your name?"

"O'Hara," the petite girl said. "Melanie O'Hara."

"The Henley?"

Kat heard her father's voice. Through the small binoculars she always carried, she saw him walking through the crowd of the familiar square, his phone held to his ear, oblivious to the fact that his only daughter was standing in the bell tower of the church, watching everything.

"That's a nice way to greet your daughter. No 'Hi, honey, how's school?'" she teased.

Her father kept his left hand shoved in his pocket, deep inside his cashmere coat, and Kat couldn't help thinking that it had got a lot colder in the past week.

"The Henley?" he asked again. "You know, someone said that my daughter was going to" – he stopped and surveyed the crowd while lowering his voice – "*rob the Henley,* but that can't be. My daughter is at the Colgan School."

"Dad, I—"

"Leave the Henley alone, Kat," he blurted. "Take a test. Go to a pep rally or—"

"A pep rally?"

"Kat, kiddo, you do not want to do this."

"Of course I don't *want* to, Dad," she said, too aware of how true and deep the sentiment ran. "We *have* to."

"*We?* Who exactly is *we?*"

"Hale," Kat said. Even from a block away she saw her father grimace. "Simon. Gabrielle." Kat wanted to keep her voice even, steady. "Hamish and Angus—"

"The Bagshaws?" he said, not hiding his disapproval.

"They didn't know she was a nun!"

A cold wind blew through the tower and down onto the square where her father stood.

"So that's it, huh?" her father asked. "You've got your own little heist society and now you're gonna rob the Henley." He turned and started moving down the busy street. "Call Uncle Eddie, Kat. Tell him it's over. You're out."

"You think Uncle Eddie is putting me up to this?" She watched the words wash over him. "You think he hasn't already got on a plane and told me to let *him* handle it?"

"Then *let him* handle it."

"Yeah." Kat fought back a laugh. "Because Uncle Eddie always has *your* best interest in mind."

"Kat…" Her father's voice was softer. "You stay away from Arturo Taccone. He's—"

"Coming for you."

"I'm fine, Kat."

"*Now*, Dad. You're fine now. You can get coffee and read newspapers and put on a show for whoever Interpol has following you that day. But if Taccone doesn't get his paintings back, five days from now there's going to be a moment when Interpol isn't watching and you're not thinking, and then Arturo Taccone's gonna be here and you will be *anything* but fine."

He shook his head. "You don't know that."

"I do." Kat turned away, leaned against the cold, rough stone of the tower wall as she spoke softly into the phone. "I do know, because he told me."

Kat turned back to the square in time to see the shock sweep over her father, followed quickly by fear. "You stay out of this, Kat. You stay away from—"

"It's too late, Daddy."

"What's that supposed to mean?"

When the sirens first broke through the damp chilly air that surrounded them, Bobby Bishop didn't even seem surprised. He had made his peace long before, but his daughter's conscience wasn't so clean. She shivered.

"It means you taught me well."

"Robert Bishop?" Kat heard Amelia Bennett's voice come clearly through the phone. She watched her father study the woman who was walking towards him, with her chic haircut and designer coat, and Kat knew that if it hadn't been for the badge in the woman's hand, her father would have never guessed she was a police officer. Or, more specifically, Interpol.

"Hang up the phone and put your hands behind your back, sir," a uniformed officer said, appearing at her father's side. But her father didn't move. Instead he yelled, "Don't do it, Kat."

She watched the officer reach for the phone, heard her father call out one last time, "Go back to school, Kat."

And then nothing. The scene in the square was like a movie with no sound as Kat said, "Dad," but no one heard her. The crowd parted. Sirens wailed. And high above the chaos, Kat whispered, "I'm sorry."

TWENTY-TWO

Kat used to love Paris, but as she walked away from her father that afternoon, the pavements seemed too crowded and foreign and cold. She wanted to go home. Wherever that was.

She felt someone bump against her as she waited on a street corner for the light to change. She heard a soft "Sorry," but didn't turn to acknowledge whoever had spoken her native language on that foreign street.

Of course, in the weeks that followed, Kat would look back on this decision from time to time and allow herself to feel at least a little bit stupid. She'd had a lot on her mind at that moment, it was true. She'd been worried about her father. Worried that the cops might realize that Melanie O'Hara and Katarina Bishop were one and the same, and that the eyewitness account of the former was good enough to hold the latter's father and keep him from Taccone, but not quite good enough to keep him in jail.

She'd worried what Uncle Eddie would say when he found out that she'd broken the thief's (much less the daughter's) ultimate code.

Given her current mindset, it was understandable that it was instinct alone that made Kat brush against the boy who, two seconds before, had brushed against her.

Or maybe, Kat wondered later, it was fate.

"Did she find you, sir?" the bellman said as he passed the boy on the hotel stairs.

The boy stopped. "I'm sorry?"

"The young lady, sir. She said she was your cousin." The bellman paused, concern growing on his face. "She said she had a key, sir. She knew your name and room number."

The bellman didn't notice the worry that briefly flashed in the boy's eyes.

"Oh good. She made it," the boy said calmly, as he processed the news that was anything but good.

The bellman saw the boy turn and walk casually down the hall. But he didn't see the look of shock on the boy's face when the door to room 157 swung open freely, unlocked.

The bellman certainly didn't see the girl who sat with her legs thrown over the side of a wingback chair as she cocked an eyebrow and said, "Welcome home."

* * *

The element of surprise is one of the greatest weapons at a thief's disposal, or so Kat had to think when she saw the boy's face. He stood framed in the doorway of his own hotel room, staring at her, shocked.

"What?" Kat asked, feigning ignorance. "No 'Hello'? No 'Honey, I'm home'?"

"You." He turned his head and looked down the narrow, empty hallway, as if she had just rushed inside and that was how she'd got into his room.

"I don't believe we were properly introduced on the street." Kat swung her legs off the silk-upholstered arm. "I'm Katarina Bishop. But you already know that if you looked in the wallet you've got in the inside left pocket of that coat you're wearing." He touched his pocket as if checking to see whether or not she was correct. She was.

"My friends call me Kat." She looked the boy up and down. "I'm not sure what you should call me."

At the end of the hall, a television blared. Kat heard a French anchorwoman announcing the arrest of a suspect in the robbery of a local gallery where a valuable statue had been stolen. She flinched and hoped the boy didn't notice.

"How'd you get in here?"

She raised her eyebrows. "You can pick pockets." Kat

watched his hand fly to his back pocket. "I can pick locks. Looking for this?" she asked, holding up his wallet. "Oops. Maybe I can pick pockets too."

She held his wallet towards him. "Care to trade?" Then she opened it and looked at the ID. "Nicholas Smith. Sixteen. British citizen." She glanced between the I.D. and the boy in front of her. "Not very photogenic."

She hopped from her chair and plucked her own wallet from his limp hands. She tossed his onto the hotel bed.

"How…" he started, but Kat's look stopped him.

"You're telegraphing your cover," she said matter-of-factly.

Kat was prepared for an argument and lies – anything but the sight of the boy smiling, the sound of him saying, "Wow. Talented *and* cute. It's very nice to meet you, Katarina." The boy dropped onto the corner of the bed and pulled off one shoe. "How old are you, anyway?" Kat didn't answer.

She turned instead and fingered the fresh flowers on the table, eyed the silk window coverings blocking the view. "This is a nice place. You pay for it working short cons?"

The boy looked up at her. He had short dark hair and bright blue eyes and the kind of smile that made you forget what you'd been thinking. "Among other things."

"And you've been practising for" – Kat eyed him again – "two years?" she guessed. The pleased look on his face was answer enough. "Where did you learn?"

"Around." He shrugged. "You pick up things. You practise."

Kat had been picking things up since her third birthday, when Hamish and Angus's father took them all to the circus because he needed to "borrow" an elephant.

"You ever get caught?" she asked, and he shrugged again.

"Not by the police."

"Do you have a record?" He shook his head. "Do you have a crew?" she asked.

"I work alone."

Kat wondered whether or not the boy who had bumped into her on a Paris street was as good as she thought he might be. And whether or not he knew it.

She studied him, wondering if the missing piece of her plan might have strolled into her life. "Do you want to keep it that way?"

4 DAYS
UNTIL DEADLINE

WYNDHAM MANOR,
ENGLAND

TWENTY-THREE

Of all the things that should have fallen within Katarina Bishop's comfort zone, sneaking into a mansion (especially this particular mansion) at three o'clock in the morning should have been incredibly high on the list. After all, she knew the pros and cons of the security system (because she'd been the one to recommend it). She was familiar with the house and was well aware of the fact that the patio doors were painted shut and the rosebushes beneath the dining room windows were equipped with a particularly nasty supply of thorns.

But that night, walking through the front door of the Hale estate felt a lot like walking back into Uncle Eddie's kitchen – like she'd left without permission, and she might never really belong inside again.

So she tried to cling to the shadows. She wanted everyone to be asleep.

"Kat?"

She froze and cursed the creaky floors.

"Kat, is that you?" Gabrielle's voice was high and scratchy. Despite the darkness, Kat could easily make out her cousin sitting at the top of the stairs. Her arms were wrapped around her knees. Her hair was pulled into a sloppy mess on the top of her head.

"What is it?" Kat asked. "What's wrong? Is it Taccone? Did he—"

"It's your dad, Kat. He was arrested."

A light turned on in one of the rooms upstairs, and Kat heard voices approaching.

She looked at Gabrielle, praying she would understand. "I know."

"You did what?"

Kat wasn't sure who said it first, because it seemed like her entire crew had blurted out the question at the exact same time. She wasn't even sure where to look, because every eye in the billiards room was staring at her with such heat and scrutiny, it was like squinting at the sun.

"I made an executive decision," Kat told them.

"So *you* went to the police?" Simon said as if he'd plugged that piece of intelligence into his monster mind and the data didn't quite compute.

"Interpol, actually." Kat managed a casual shrug. "Technically, I went to Interpol."

"And you ratted on your dad?" Angus asked.

"He's better off where he is. Trust me," she said.

"But you're his daughter, Kat." Hamish's eyes were wide. "Uncle Eddie's gonna kill you."

"I'm also the girl who's trying to *undo* the only Pseudonima job ever done in our lifetime, Hamish. Not even Uncle Eddie can kill me twice."

Simon dropped to the sofa. "I don't think I'd do well in prison."

Kat tried not to notice the way Hamish and Angus gripped their pool cues, or the way Gabrielle sat quietly beside the window, a worried expression on her face.

"Guys, I—"

"She did the right thing." They were the words she never expected to hear, from the one person she never expected to say them. Hale dropped onto an ottoman. "If this doesn't work, and" – he almost smiled – "it'd kinda be a miracle for it to work...then your dad's gonna need as much standing between him and Arturo Taccone as possible."

He looked at Kat. Something stretched out between them in that moment, and she knew that no one would deny Hale – or doubt him. That no one would fight them both. And so maybe they could have left it at that. Maybe the tension would have blown over if an unfamiliar boy hadn't chosen that moment to appear in the doorway and say, "Hello."

Simon lunged for a laptop that sat open on the wet bar and shut it with a snap. Hamish threw a coat over the model of the Henley that lay on the floor beside the sofa, but Hale didn't make a single move. He just looked at the boy in the doorway and back at Kat.

"Who's this guy?" he asked, jerking his head towards the boy extending his hand.

"Hi, I'm Nick. Kat told me—"

"To wait outside," Kat warned.

"So?" Hale asked, still staring at Kat.

"Nick's a pocket man. He and I…*bumped* into each other in Paris." Kat wanted to sound sure and in control – like someone who deserved to be there. "Nick, this is Gabrielle." Her cousin gave the faintest hint of a wave with two fingers. "The Bagshaws, Angus and Hamish. Simon – I told you about him. And this is Hale," Kat finished. "Hale's—"

"Hale's wondering exactly what *Nick's* doing here."

Kat listened for the familiar teasing in Hale's voice, but she knew he wasn't even the tiniest bit amused.

"You said it yourself, Hale." Kat lowered her voice. "We need one more."

"Two more," Hale corrected. "Actually, I said we needed two more, and he—"

"He's in," Kat said flatly. "We can do it with seven. And he's in."

Kat looked at her crew: Angus was the oldest, Simon was the smartest, Gabrielle was the quickest, and Hamish was the strongest. But Hale was the only one willing to say what everyone else was thinking.

"I knew it," he said, turning away. "I knew I should have gone with you. First you tell some phoney story about your dad to the police—"

"Interpol," Hamish, Angus, and Simon all corrected.

"And then you come home with this?" Hale snapped, pointing at Nick as if the boy couldn't hear. As if Kat were an amateur. A fool.

Kat shook her head, wishing she could say for certain that he was wrong.

"Can I see you outside for a second?" Kat glared at Hale, then walked to the patio doors and out onto the veranda.

As Hale closed the door behind him, Kat heard Angus say, "Ooh, Mom and Dad are going to fight now."

* * *

Outside, the air was cool. She wished she'd brought a coat, that Hale would put his arm around her and tease her for bringing home strays and lost causes. But his tone was anything but warm. "You're too close to this one, Kat. You're way too involved to think—"

"I know," she practically yelled. "I *am* close. This is my life, Hale. Mine. My father. My job. My responsibility."

"Clearly." He sounded so calm and detached. Everything she wasn't.

"I know what I'm doing, Hale."

"Really? Because I could swear that in the past twenty-four hours you've turned your father in—"

"Five minutes ago you thought that was a great idea," she reminded him. He pushed on.

"—to the cops, and brought home a stranger."

"Nick's good, Hale. He picked me clean and I never saw it coming."

Hale shook his head. "This is a bad call, Kat. If Uncle Eddie were here—"

"Uncle Eddie's *not* here," she snapped. "Uncle Eddie isn't going to be here." Her voice cracked, but Hale either didn't hear or didn't care.

"Uncle Eddie would stop you."

Kat looked at him, read the cool indifference in his eyes. "So that's what you're going to do?" she asked. "Stop me?"

She wanted him to say, "Of course not," but instead, he looked her right in the eye and said, "Maybe I should." He stepped closer. "This guy is—"

"What, Hale?" Kat shouted, louder now. "What is he exactly?"

"He's not part of the family."

"Yeah, well—" Kat sighed. "Neither are you."

Katarina Bishop was a criminal. But she'd never held a gun. She'd never thrown a punch. Until that moment she didn't really know how it felt to hurt someone, and as soon as she saw the look on Hale's face, she wanted to take the words back.

And she wished she could make them hurt more.

Both. So she went inside, unable to do either.

TWENTY-FOUR

Gregory Reginald Wainwright was still relatively new to the Henley. Oh, nine months had been more than enough time for his personal effects to find their way out of boxes and onto shelves. In that time, he'd managed to learn the names of almost all of the guards and docents who worked between the hours of ten and six. But the honeymoon period, as they say, was almost over for the Henley's new director. It would not be long until the board of directors started asking to see his quarterly reports, questioning him about donation levels, budget overages, and, of course, about the man named Visily Romani.

These were the worries that filled his mind, pulling his concentration away from his newspaper that Friday morning. Perhaps that was why he didn't mind the distraction when the intercom on his desk began to buzz.

"Mr Wainwright," his assistant said, "there's a young man here who would like a few moments of your time."

He groaned. The Henley was always filled with young men. Young women, too. Which was nothing more than a polite way of saying *children*. They spilled soft drinks in the café and left fingerprints on the glass in the atrium. They filled his museum by the busload every day of the school year, crowding the exhibits, talking too loudly, and driving the Henley's director to the sanctuary of his office with his tea and his paper.

"Mr Wainwright?" The assistant's voice seemed more urgent now. "Shall I show the young man in? He doesn't have an appointment, but he was hoping you might take a moment for him."

Gregory Wainwright was searching for an answer – an excuse – but before he could claim to be expecting an urgent visitor or about to make an important call, his secretary added, "His name is W. W. Hale the Fifth."

"Is he good?" Nick's breath was warm against Kat's ear. They were standing too close, she thought, as they looked through the halls of the Henley toward an unmarked door where two corridors came to a T-shaped intersection. Someone will notice, Kat worried. Someone might think something. And still he stood behind her, watching, as the door to the director's private office opened, and a slightly balding, slightly paunchy, slightly awkward man emerged with a boy who was his opposite in almost every way.

Kat watched Hale make a show of holding the door open for the older man to walk through. She doubted that anyone but a seasoned professional would notice the small piece of tape he'd left on the latch, the quick glance he'd sent in her direction.

And then she exhaled and said, "Yeah. He's good." But what she thought was, *He's still angry.*

The director removed a small card from the inside pocket of his suit jacket, then swiped it through an electronic reader. The Henley has state-of-the-art security, the gesture said. The Henley's art is the safest art in the world, no matter what you might have read in the paper.

But, of course, he didn't know about Hale and his duct tape.

As the man returned the card to his jacket, Kat turned to Nick.

"You got it?" she asked. He nodded.

"Inside left pocket." Nick slouched forwards and grinned a sloppy grin. "Lucky I'm left-handed."

"Luck, my friend, has absolutely nothing to do with it." Gabrielle's voice was even as she passed. There was no flirt, no ditz. She was all business as she teetered to the end of the corridor and called, "If you'll follow me, please." Instantly the small speaker in Kat's ear was alive with noise. It sounded like a flock of birds was nesting in her head – cawing and screeching – as one hundred and fifty chattering school children gathered behind Gabrielle and followed her back down the small corridor.

The noise was deafening. Kat and Nick pushed themselves against the wall, out of the way of the kids in their neatly pressed trousers and navy blazers.

"We're sorry for the inconvenience," Gabrielle was yelling to the teachers at the front of the mob. "Today we're starting all tours in the sculpture garden."

Through her earpiece, over the roar of the children, Kat heard Hale chattering to the director about London. About rain. About his unyielding search for the perfect fish and chips. The guards at the end of the hall were pressing themselves to the wall, their duties forgotten in the chaos that flowed in Gabrielle's wake.

"Angus, Simon, you're clear," Kat whispered.

The guards didn't see the unmarked door push easily open. The kids in the pack didn't notice when the two boys no one had ever seen before suddenly disappeared from their midst.

"We're in," Angus said into Kat's ear a second later. The kids kept walking, moving through the Henley's halls like a tide, but when Kat turned to leave, she walked in the opposite direction. She wasn't an ordinary kid, after all.

Katarina Bishop followed no one.

"The way I hear it, there *was* a Visily Romani once."

"Just watch the door, Hamish," Kat warned.

"I'm on it, Kitty, don't you worry. But as I was saying, this Romani bloke was the best thief in the land, he was. Until he fell off a guard tower—"

"I heard he drowned." Angus's voice filled Kat's ear, cutting off his brother.

"I'm telling this story."

"Simon?" Kat asked as she looked around the bustling halls. "How much longer?"

"Fifteen minutes," was Simon's answer.

"But Romani didn't really die, see?" Hamish went on, undaunted. "Well, strictly speaking, he *did* die, but—"

"Hamish, are you watching the door or aren't you?" Gabrielle snapped, joining the conversation as she followed Hale and the Henley's esteemed director from a respectable distance.

"I am, love. It's clear as a bell. So anyway, as I was saying, he died, but he got reincarnated, see? Every generation there's a *new* Romani."

"That's not how it goes, Hamish," Kat tried to clarify.

"Yeah," Angus said, ever the older brother. "The original Romani drowned. And it's every *other* generation."

"Guys," Kat warned. Then something stopped her. She couldn't scold the Bagshaws – could barely speak at all – when she realized how close Nick was standing, looking at her like she had never been looked at before.

"So, Nick, have you lived in Paris long?" She stepped away from the statue they'd been pretending to admire, glad of somewhere to go.

The boy shrugged as he fell into step beside her. "Off and on." Kat felt a pang of something – annoyance, maybe? But maybe something else.

"Your accent isn't one hundred percent British, though. Is it?" Kat asked.

"My father was American. But my mom is English."

"And is she going to be missing you now?"

Nick glanced around the Henley's pristine statue collection and shook his head. "I've got a few days."

"That's all we need," Kat told him.

Nick stopped midstride and smiled at her. "Well then, that's what you'll get, Ms Bishop."

His words startled her. Or maybe it wasn't the words themselves, but the way he'd said them. She studied him, trying to see every angle.

"Oh," he said, that same cryptic smile on his face. He started walking again, just a tourist. Just a boy. "You really didn't expect me to look you up? To figure out that you were *the* Katarina Bishop?"

"Exactly how does one 'look me up'?" Kat felt herself blush, but she wasn't really sure why.

"Just because I work alone doesn't mean I don't have resources. Only, rumour has it you'd walked away from the life."

"I'm not..." Kat shook her head, then tried again, stronger now. "I'm still walking."

And she was, down the grand promenade, through the crowds that had begun to thin, more equally distributed among the museum's many exhibits. As they passed the Renaissance room, Kat noticed that it wasn't neglected anymore. Tourists had gathered in front of da Vinci's final masterpiece as if the world were righting itself, settling back into place.

"And here we have Leonardo da Vinci's *Angel Returning to Heaven*," a docent was saying ten feet away. "Purchased in 1946 by Veronica Henley herself, it is widely considered one of the most valuable works of art in the world – the *most* valuable, according to Mrs Henley. When reporters asked her shortly before her death which piece she would rather have for her collection, this painting or the *Mona Lisa*, Mrs Henley said, 'Let the Louvre keep Leonardo's lady; I have his angel.'"

The tour group moved on, and Kat eased towards the da Vinci. "You tempted?" Nick asked.

Was it beautiful? Yes. Was it valuable? Incredibly. But as she stood looking at one of the most important paintings in the world, Kat couldn't help but marvel at how little temptation she felt.

And not because it was an almost impossible target, or because it would be practically impossible to resell, even on the black market.

It wasn't for any of the reasons that a good thief might list. Her reasons, Kat decided – or maybe just hoped – were those of a good person.

"You've had big scores before, though, right?" Nick asked.

Kat shrugged. "*Big* is a relative term."

"But you and your dad did the Tokyo Exchange Centre last year, right?" Kat smiled but didn't answer. "The Embassy job in Paris... The—"

"What's your real question, Nick?"

It took a minute for him to shake his head and say, "Why the Colgan job?"

"It wasn't a *job*. It was more like a...life?" Nick stared

at Kat blankly, so she added, "A way of expanding my educational horizons."

Nick laughed. "What could someone like you possibly learn at a place like that? Those kids are just...kids."

"Yeah." Kat walked on. "That was kind of the point."

"You see, Mr Hale, this is the wing your Monet would call home." Hale watched the way Gregory Wainwright held his arms out wide, as if the entire wall could be his for the taking. Hale had seen that gesture before, of course. That gesture alone was possibly why he found *taking* so very appealing.

"We have hosted some of the finest works from some of the world's finest families," the director went on while Hale turned and surveyed the gorgeous space as if he were bored. He oozed indifference. It felt almost too easy – the role he'd been born to play, after all. But then the director glanced at his watch and said, "Oh, will you look at the time," and Hale felt the director's interest slipping.

"Tell me, Mr... Worthington," Hale said, pointing at a very nice Manet, "what kind of assurances do I have that my painting wouldn't be damaged in any way?"

The director actually chuckled as he turned and glanced at the boy beside him. "We're the Henley, young man. We use only the most state-of-the-art protection measures—"

"Docents or guards in the room at all times when the building is open?"

"Yes."

"International Museum Federation anti-elements protocols?" Hale asked as the man gravitated toward the exit. "Gold level?"

The director looked insulted. "Level Platinum."

"Magnetic tags tied to sensors at every conceivable exit?"

"*Of course.*" The director stopped. For the first time since he'd met the young man, Gregory Wainwright dared to look at him as if he were merely just another annoying teenager. "In fact, speaking of protection, I'm afraid I have a rather urgent ten o'clock meeting with our head of security."

Through his earpiece, Hale heard Kat ask what he really wanted to know. "You ready for company, Simon?"

"Five minutes," Simon answered from a wing away.

The director talked on. "I can assure you, our acquisitions department is used to accommodating almost any request, so if you're ready to begin the paperwork, perhaps we should—"

"Oh, I'm not here to start the paperwork." Hale stopped in the centre of the director's path, stalling as he appraised a very nice Pissarro in a way that said he had paintings twice that nice at home. Which, in fact, he did.

The museum director laughed uncomfortably. "I'm sorry, sir. I was under the impression that you would like to place your family's Monet on temporary exhibit at the Henley."

"No," Hale said simply, stepping in front of the man, stopping him, but only for a moment. "I don't *want* to place my family's Monet at the Henley."

"I'm sorry, Mr Hale. I'm afraid I'm quite confused, sir. You're here because..." the director prodded.

"Of Kat," Hale finished the man's sentence as he glanced up and down the corridor at where Kat and Nick stood gaping twenty feet away. But Gregory Wainwright just kept nodding, waiting for the young billionaire to finish. "I'm here because of her."

Perhaps most middle-aged businessmen would have balked at such an unusual statement from an anything-but-usual boy, but Gregory Wainwright was accustomed to the odd ways of the oddly wealthy, so he nodded. He smiled as he asked, "Cats, you say?"

"Yeah," Hale said, and Kat couldn't help but observe

that Hale was becoming a fairly decent inside man. When he stayed on script, that is. Unfortunately for everyone, Hale was never on script. And worse, Gregory Wainwright had started walking, forcing Hale to follow.

"You see, Greg, my mother is going through a feline phase. Binky is a Persian," Hale said simply, as if that should explain everything. "Binky has a nasty habit of shedding all over the living room furniture, you see." Gregory Wainwright nodded as if he understood perfectly.

"And so we had to get new living room furniture, which, unfortunately, does not go with the Monet."

Kat stood for a moment, staring into that small window of the world where someone would tire of a Monet simply because it clashed with the sofa.

But perhaps the strangest part was that, to Gregory Wainwright, and indeed to Hale himself, the story didn't ring strange at all. Kat thought about Hale's mother's empty room and empty house – all the valuable things in her life that the woman never thought to miss

"He *is* good." Nick looked at Kat, who couldn't help but smile. "How long have you two been together?" Nick asked, and just that quickly, Kat wasn't smiling anymore.

"We're not together," Kat blurted. Instantly, she wished she'd said something different. Something coy. Something clever. But it was too late, and she was stuck sounding like a silly girl and a very bad liar – two things she had never been before.

"I meant, how long have you been *working* together?" he corrected. Then he smiled his slightly goofy smile. "But that's good to know, too."

Before she could even ponder that statement, footsteps began to echo in the hallway that led to the director's private office.

"Simon?" Kat questioned, but before the boy had even finished his "Just one more minute!" something happened that Kat had never experienced on any job of any kind.

The director and Hale were fast approaching, and to Kat's surprise, so was Nick.

"Stall," she whispered, starting to turn, to think, to work.

But just as quickly, Nick was grasping her arm, pulling him back to her with a quiet, "OK." And before a single diversionary tactic could come to mind, she was in Nick's arms, and he was kissing her right there in the middle of the Henley's hallway.

Right there in front of Gregory Wainwright and Hale.

She was aware, faintly, of the two of them skidding to a stop before they could turn the corner – and catch Simon in the act. She was certain she heard the director mutter something that sounded a great deal like "Children kissing in my halls…"

Through her earpiece, she heard Angus say, "We're clear." But the voice Kat most wanted to hear was Hale's.

She pulled away from Nick right as Hale said, perfectly casual, completely unfazed, "To tell you the truth, Mr Wainwright, before I can promise you anything, I would really like to hear from you that there's nothing to fear from this man" – he snapped his fingers as if trying to remember the name – "Visily Romani."

TWENTY-FIVE

Despite rumours to the contrary, Mrs W. W. Hale III had not added a large solarium to the Hale family's English estate because it was fashionable at the time, or to keep up with Mrs Winthrop Covington II, who had built a similar addition to her manor house three miles away. No, Hale's grandmother had ordered the construction of that particular room for two primary reasons: One, she hated to be cold. And two, she dearly loved the Henley's massive glass-covered foyer.

As Kat sat with her crew in the glass-enclosed space that evening, eating soup and sandwiches, discussing all they'd learned, Kat wondered if anyone besides her was impressed with the irony. Probably not, she decided.

"How's it coming, Simon?" Gabrielle asked.

Simon, completely enthralled by the small electronic gizmos and wires that covered the table, took a moment to answer.

"We have eyes." He turned the computer around, and there, in living colour and from a quite unflattering angle, was Gregory Wainwright.

"Mr Wainwright?" a high, female voice cut through the air. Simon beamed.

"And ears."

"Nice work, Simon," Gabrielle said with a kiss on his cheek.

"I helped," Hamish reminded her, moving his cheek in her direction, but Gabrielle wasn't feeling quite that liberal with her affection.

"Mr Wainwright?" The secretary's voice came through the intercom, and the man on the screen moved. Lurched, really.

"He's napping," Gabrielle said with a laugh.

"So what do we need to know about him, Hale?" Kat said. "Besides the fact that he likes to doze off in his office."

"He's a suit. He's concerned with typical suit stuff," Hale said, clearly an expert on the subject. "Donations, revenue streams" – Hale paused, and even the Bagshaw boys stopped to listen – "publicity."

Glass surrounded them on three sides. Perfectly tended plants sprawled throughout the space, and Kat felt the high that comes from too much oxygen and possibility.

"Our friend Romani has made life for Mr Wainwright very, very difficult," Hale said with a smile. He leaned back in a wrought-iron chair, which Kat guessed was as old as the glass dome around them. "The official party line is what we've already heard – a prank, a mistake by the caretaking staff – the usual stuff."

"But unofficially?" Angus asked.

Hale nodded. "The Henley is spooked."

On the screen, the secretary was entering the office. She held a small pad of paper in her hands, was rattling off something about a black-tie fund-raiser, a faulty furnace, a new record for attendance, and the annual evaluation of the building's fire codes. And through it all, Gregory Wainwright kept nodding impatiently, desperate to return to his nap.

"Scared..." Kat started. She stood. It felt very good to stretch, and as she walked, she asked herself how her father would rob the Henley. And then Uncle Eddie. And then, finally, her mother. But there was only one thief who had ever done what she was trying to undo, so in the end Kat tried to think like Visily Romani.

"We're making it too hard," Kat said, more for her own benefit than anyone else's. "We're not stealing *from* the Henley. We're stealing *at* the Henley." She began to pace in long strides.

"They're scared," she said, stopping, turning to Hale. "Right?"

He nodded slowly and leaned forwards, elbows on knees, and something in the gesture reminded Kat of her father. She pointed to the plans. "Then we give them reason to be *terrified*."

An awed silence filled the room as five of the greatest junior thieves the world would ever know stared at her and uttered, "Smokey the Bear."

"It could work," Simon said, nodding slowly.

"It will work," Gabrielle added.

Angus even raised his hand, as if Kat were a visiting professor. "Yeah, well that still doesn't explain how we're going to carry five paintings out of the most secure museum in the world—"

"Even if they aren't *their* paintings," Hamish reminded them again.

"Without getting noticed," his brother finished.

Kat walked to the window. She tried to see out into the night, but the glass had become a mirror in the darkness. Kat stared at their reflections, studied them all in turn.

"So we get noticed."

To call it a party would be a mistake. It wasn't a celebration so much as an excuse to blow off steam. But when Hamish found an old phonograph and a collection of ragtime records in the corner of the solarium, there was no doubt the music changed things.

Maybe it was the scratchy sound of trumpets reverberating off the glass – maybe they were all a little drunk on the possibility (or perhaps the illusion) that this thing might actually work. But, eventually, Simon asked Gabrielle to dance, and proved he was surprisingly good. Angus challenged Hamish to balance a cricket bat on his chin for two minutes (which he did).

And, through it all, Kat sat on an old chaise longue, watching the party. Hale sat on the other side of the room, watching her.

"So does he hate everyone, or am I special?" Kat didn't have to turn. She could see Nick standing over her shoulder, reflected in the glass. He threw one leg over the chaise longue and sank onto the cushion beside her. She felt suddenly conspicuous, as if there were entirely too much *them* and too little *chair*.

Hale looked away.

"You never did answer my question, you know," Nick said. He took a sip from his drink. "This afternoon?" He cocked his head in Hale's direction. "How long have you two been...together?"

Kat pulled her legs under her, farther from him.

"Oh, a while," she said, and then for reasons Kat would never know, she couldn't stop herself from smiling at the memory.

There are stories thieves don't tell – trade secrets, mostly. Or incriminating tales. Or mistakes too embarrassing to repeat. The story of Kat and Hale was none of those things, and yet it was one she never said aloud; at that moment she wondered why. She studied him across the room. He smiled back in a way that said, despite the music and distance, somehow he'd heard – somehow he was thinking the exact same thing.

Hamish's right arm was around Angus's waist as the two of them tangoed past.

"I still vote for Uncle Felix," Hamish was saying.

"Did the man on that tape look like he had a bum leg to you?" Angus asked, his cheek pressed against his brother's.

"Uncle Felix hurt his leg?" Kat asked, and Hamish shuddered.

"Alligators," he said, stopping midstride. "They're faster than they look."

The Bagshaws both seemed to be studying her.

"Smile, Kat," Angus told her. "It's a good plan. Uncle Eddie couldn't have done better."

Hamish raised an imaginary glass. "To Uncle Eddie."

Everyone echoed the toast, except for the boy beside her. "Who's Uncle Eddie?"

Perhaps it was her imagination, but Kat could have sworn that the needle on the phonograph skipped. For a moment, everyone stopped dancing.

While the whole crew stared at Nick, Hale smirked at Kat, challenging her to describe the indescribable.

"Uncle Eddie is...my uncle." Kat started like every good con starts, with a little bit of the truth.

Gabrielle added, "*Our* uncle."

"*Yes, Gabrielle*," Kat conceded. "Uncle Eddie is our grandfather's brother. He is *our* great-uncle." She gestured to herself and Gabrielle. "The real kind."

"Way to rub it in, Kat," Angus said with only a semi-mocking tone as he and his brother danced by. (Kat wasn't sure who was leading.)

"The Bagshaws are sort of like..." Kat struggled with the words.

"Our grandfather worked with Eddie before he even moved to New York," Angus explained.

"You ever hear of the Dublin Doxy Heist?" Hamish asked, eyes wide. "What about the time someone ransomed that little dog Queen Elizabeth was gonna breed all her other dogs with?"

"And then she got the wrong dog back?" his brother

finished. Nick shook his head.

The brothers shrugged as if Nick were utterly beyond saving, and resumed their tango. Nick turned to Simon, unfazed. "How about you? How do you know this Uncle Eddie?"

Simon rubbed his hands together. "My dad had a sort of cash-flow problem when he was at MIT, and that's how he met—"

"My grandfather," Gabrielle interjected as she reached for Simon's hands and pulled him to his feet.

"*Our* grandfather," Kat corrected as Simon tried to dip Gabrielle. And failed.

"Who was Eddie's brother," Simon said, reaching for the girl who was currently sprawled across a hard floor for the second time in three days.

Across the room, Hale smiled slightly. "We can draw you a diagram if you need it."

"No thanks," Nick said. "I think I've got everyone but you."

"Oh." Hale smirked. "That's simple." Kat wasn't moving – wasn't dancing – and yet it felt like her heart might pound out of her chest as she watched Hale lean farther into the shadows and say, "I'm the guy who happened to be home the night Kat came to steal a Monet."

TWENTY-SIX

Hale found her in the garden, staring at a statue of Prometheus that W. W. Hale the First had purchased in Greece and transplanted to Wyndham Manor sometime before the first World War.

"I wouldn't try stealing that, if I were you." His voice came from behind her, but Kat didn't turn.

"The weight would make it hard," she said.

From the corner of her eye, she saw Hale stop beside her, hands shoved into pockets, looking up. "You'd need a crane," he said. "Cranes are loud."

"And big."

"They leave nasty tracks all over gardens." Kat could almost feel him smile. "And quads."

Not for the first time, Kat wanted to ask about Colgan and the Porsche and exactly how he'd done it, but every good thief knows that the only job that matters is the next job. So Kat stayed quiet in the midst of the rosebushes and fountains and perfectly trimmed hedges that ran across three acres like a maze. She stood at the centre of it, not at all surprised that he'd found her.

"He stole fire from the gods," she said flatly, pointing at the statue.

Hale sighed. "The Visily Romani of his time."

In comparison, even Arturo Taccone didn't seem like such a threat. The music had been turned up and was floating through the glass and out into the night. Inside, someone was laughing. And Katarina Bishop was standing with Hale in the chilly air, watching his foggy breath.

Hale's hand found hers. It was big and warm around her cold fingers. It felt like it belonged there. And then, just that quickly, it was gone, and Kat found herself grasping crisp, cold paper.

"I found these, by the way." Hale studied Kat's face as she looked down at the manila envelope that she had hoped to never see again.

"How did you..."

"Under the rug in your bedroom, Kat? Really?" He laughed. "For an excellent thief, you really are a terrible hider." She didn't open the envelope. She already knew too well what was inside. "The one of me is especially nice." He turned his head. "It captured my good side."

"I didn't notice you had one."

He smiled. "Oh, I think you noticed." He stepped closer. They were almost touching as he said, "A little bit."

"Hale—"

"If I kill Taccone, would that help your dad?" Hale asked, and Kat was too tired to gauge if he was joking. "Marcus would do it," he added. "I've always told him his job description was up for modification. Or Gabrielle? She's got this nail file – thing's like a switchblade."

"And you've seen a lot of switchblades on Martha's Vineyard?"

"Hey, the Yacht Club loves a good rumble."

It was funny. He was funny. Kat wanted to laugh. She tried to will herself to do it. To dance. To be the girl she'd tried – and failed – to be at Colgan.

But instead she inched away from the very kind, very funny, very handsome boy who had followed her into the dark, somehow bringing the music with him.

"Why are you doing this, Hale?"

"What?" he said. He was still too close.

"You could do anything," she said softly, looking down, wanting him to hear her but not see her. "Why are you doing *this?*"

His arm was warm against hers. "I always wanted to do the Henley."

"Can you be serious for a second?"

"Dance with me."

"What?" she asked, but his arms were already going around her waist. He was already holding her tightly against him.

"Dancing. Come on. You can do it. It's a lot like navigating through a laser grid. It requires rhythm." He moved her hips to the beat of the distant music. "And patience." He spun her out slowly and back towards him. "And it's only fun if you trust your partner." The dip was so slow, so smooth, that Kat didn't know it was happening until the world had already turned upside down and Hale's face was inches from her own.

"Count me in, Kat." He squeezed her tighter. "You should always count me in."

In the hours that followed, a simple kind of peace fell over Wyndham Manor.

Marcus and Nick disappeared inside their third-floor bedrooms. The Bagshaws fell asleep in the solarium while the phonograph played and the party continued in their dreams. Gabrielle did her nails and, for practice, picked Simon's pocket – twice – before going upstairs and crawling into bed.

Only two members of the party did not find easy sleep.

Kat sat at the base of the stairs for a long time, looking

at the pictures, reminding herself of exactly what was at stake.

Uncle Eddie was on his favourite bench. Gabrielle was still more beautiful than any one person ever had the right to be. And Hale was right, Kat had to admit: Taccone's picture really did capture his good side.

But it was the picture of her father that Kat looked at the longest. She studied the familiar square, the people in the crowd. Amelia Bennett was there, in the background, and somehow Kat felt relieved, remembering that someone was still watching over her father, even if she couldn't. But then Kat saw someone else.

She fought the urge to curse or feel like a fool. Instead she sat quietly and said, "Oh boy."

Hale was the only other person still awake. He'd gone into the pantry and closed the door. Standing among the cans of tomato sauce and bags of flour, he pulled out his phone and dialled a number.

"Uncle Eddie," Hale said slowly. He took a deep breath. "I think I need your help. Who do we know in Paris?"

3 DAYS
UNTIL DEADLINE

WYNDHAM MANOR,
ENGLAND

TWENTY-SEVEN

In her dream, Kat heard the music. It was louder there, away from the garden, echoing off the glass walls and tiled floors. She looked for Hale, but he was gone, lost among the Henley's crowd. She craned her neck, searching. But the sun streaming into the room was too bright; the music was too loud. And yet, no one was dancing.

"Hale!" Kat called. "Gabrielle!"

Something was wrong, Kat knew, but it was too late to stop it...to stop...*something*.

"Hale!" she called again, but his name was drowned out by the sound that echoed through the atrium: a roar like thunder, followed by a flash of lightning. But outside there was only sun – no clouds, no storm. And yet inside it was raining. A dark cloud formed, blocking out the light as people ran and cried and screamed. But Kat stood still beneath the pouring rain, staring through the parting crowd at a woman near the entrance in a bright red coat and patent leather shoes, staring back at her.

"Mom?" Kat's voice was barely audible over the approaching police sirens, the museum's blaring alarms. "Mom!" Kat cried again. She pushed against the sea of bodies, following the woman outside.

And just that quickly, the sun was gone. Night had fallen. The rain began to freeze, and her mother's red coat stood out against the white blanket of snow that covered the city's streets.

"Mom!" Kat called, but the woman didn't turn. "Mom, wait for me!"

Kat ran faster, trying not to fall, but the snow was too deep; her hands grew cold. And in the distance the alarms were still ringing.

I should hide, she thought. I should run. But instead she followed in the woman's footsteps, searching for the red door, the red coat.

"Mom!" The snow was coming faster now, covering the footprints. "Mom, come back!"

Snowflakes clung to her lashes, ran down her face like tears, while the sirens grew louder, closer, pulling Kat from a dream she didn't want to leave. She reached out as if there were a way to hold on to the snow, to the night. But the noise was too loud. Kat opened her eyes – she knew her mother was gone and she could not follow.

She reached for her bedside table and turned off her alarm. She closed her eyes, hoping the dream wasn't gone for good. But her room was already bathed in rare rays of British sunlight; her duvet was heavy and warm, tucked around her in the soft bed. Kat thought of the woman in the red coat, and knew why she hadn't waited.

There are some places daughters aren't supposed to follow.

So Kat rolled onto her back, stared at the ornate ceiling, then sighed and said, "Phase three."

When Kat finally made her way downstairs, Marcus was standing to attention beside the open patio doors, a plate of toast in one hand, a walkie-talkie in the other. Simon sat at the centre of a long table, surrounded by laptops and wires. But it was Nick who drew Kat's attention as he sat at the head of the table, flanked on either side by Hale and Gabrielle.

"Don't ever ask a question when the answer is no," Hale told him.

"Don't ever break character – not even for a second," Gabrielle added.

"You should always be in control of the conversation," Hale said.

"Your mark should always *think* he's in control of the

conversation," Gabrielle said in turn.

Kat knew that speech. Kat had *given* that speech.

"And never, ever—" Hale started, but Nick had turned towards Kat, smiling.

"Good morning." He seemed utterly at home, at ease. "Someone got her beauty sleep."

Gabrielle looked at Kat's wild hair and wrinkled pyjamas. "That's not exactly beauty." She smirked at her cousin. "No offence."

Before Kat could respond, spirals of dark smoke swirled up from behind the long stone fences that crisscrossed through the fields in the distance, and a scratchy voice boomed from Marcus's hand.

"How was that?" Angus sounded entirely too pleased with himself.

Gabrielle gestured upwards with her thumb, so Marcus pressed the talk button on the walkie-talkie and said, "Bigger."

Nick glanced at Hale. "Don't you have neighbours?" he asked.

Hale ignored him. Instead, he leaned closer to Kat. "He isn't ready," he told her. "*I* should do this."

Kat shook her head. "Wainwright knows your voice."

"I can do the accent."

Kat smiled. "Like you did the accent in Hong Kong?"

Hale exhaled loudly. "I can do the accent *better* this time."

"No." Kat didn't feel like arguing.

"Thanks for the vote of confidence, love," Nick said in the perfect accent of the native Londoner that he was.

She saw Hale start to speak, to challenge the new status quo, but then Simon said, "Showtime," and turned an enormous laptop around for them to see.

Anyone could tell from the image on the screen that Gregory Wainwright was not a morning person.

His tie was entirely too crooked for a man of his station. His suit was rumpled. And as he lumbered towards his desk, he looked a great deal like a man who wanted nothing more than to return to his bed.

Hale looked at Nick. "You sure you're up for this, newbie?"

"Oh," Nick said with a laugh, "thanks for the concern, but I think I'll be OK."

"Yeah," Hale scoffed. "Well, OK might be OK working short cons and street stuff, but this is…"

The walkie-talkie crackled to life again. "Excuse me, miss," Marcus said a moment later. "The gentlemen would like to know if" – he cleared his throat – "that boom was as bloody brilliant as they thought it was."

Kat hadn't heard anything but the sound of the quiet

war waging beside her, and so it fell to Gabrielle to lean towards the butler and say, "More smoke. Less boom."

Marcus dutifully relayed the message.

"Guys," Simon warned, turning down the sound and pointing to the man on the screen, who was now talking to his assistant. "It's *showtime*," he said again. But neither Nick nor Hale seemed to notice or care as they stared at each other across the table.

In the distance, Angus was chasing Hamish across the dewy grounds toward the rising, spiralling smoke, and Kat found herself whispering, "Two boys running..."

Hale looked up. Only he seemed to have heard her, and with that, he slid the phone across the table to Nick. "Make the call."

They saw Wainwright pick up the phone. They heard Nick say, "Yes, Mr Wainwright, Edward Wallace from Binder and Sloan here calling to assure you personally that this nasty business with our Windsor Elite furnace model is not as bad as you might have heard. Why, the fire marshal has assured us that—"

On screen, they saw Wainwright speak, but only Nick could hear him.

"Oh dear," Nick said with a wink in Kat's direction. "That *is* disturbing. Well, not to fear, Mr Wainwright. I'll tell you what I told Her Majesty's personal valet this morning: We at Binder and Sloan have been entrusted with the safety and comfort of some of the United Kingdom's most beloved buildings, and we will not rest until every faulty furnace has been repaired."

Wainwright stood to examine the small vents in the floor of his office as if he expected flames to come shooting out at any minute.

"Yes, sir," Nick said. "Now, I see that we can have a team come out to do these repairs two weeks from next Tuesday – Not quick enough? Of course, sir. It is a high priority, yes sir. Of course. Yes. First thing Monday it is."

Walkie-talkie static filled the air again, and Marcus said, "Excuse me, miss, but the young gentlemen say that you cannot get smoke without the boom, and they would like your advice on how to proceed."

But Kat's mind was still lost in a dream, clouded with smoke and fire.

"Excuse me," Marcus whispered. "Miss, the gentlemen—"

"Are morons," Gabrielle said, taking the walkie-talkie. Kat watched her cousin storm off with an exasperated sigh of, "I guess I have to do everything myself."

Kat, Hale, and Nick watched her go. Another roar bellowed in the distance as Kat found Hale's gaze and whispered, "Bigger."

TWENTY-EIGHT

Sometimes Katarina Bishop couldn't help but wonder if she had been the victim of some colossal, genetic mistake. After all, she almost always preferred black to pink, flats to heels, and as she stood perfectly still atop one of the silk upholstered chairs in Hale's great-great-grandmother's dressing room, all she could think was maybe she wasn't even female – at least when compared to Gabrielle.

She glanced down at her cousin, who sat on her knees beside the chair, a pincushion in one hand and a mobile in the other.

"Of course I want to come to your engagement party," Gabrielle said with a sigh into the phone. "Those are always fun, but you know how Switzerland is this time of year." She darted her eyes toward her cousin. "No, Mother, I haven't seen Kat in ages – you know we're not exactly *close*."

Gabrielle winked.

"It's too short," Kat whispered at the exact moment Gabrielle chose to mouth, *I think it's too long.*

"Sure, I think you should call Uncle Eddie," Gabrielle said into the phone, but stared up, straight into her cousin's eyes. "Whoever ratted out Kat's dad should totally pay."

Kat cut her a look. Gabrielle gestured and mouthed the word *Turn.*

Kat did as she was told. She could feel her hemline rising as her cousin worked, but she didn't protest. After all, Kat was a natural grease man, wheel man, and inside man. Gabrielle was a natural girl. So Kat stayed still and quiet on her chair, staring through the bay windows, looking out onto the garden and the statue, trying to remember which parts of the night before had been a dream.

"So…" Gabrielle said slowly. The mobile was gone. The skirt was nearly finished. And there was no disguising the thrill in her voice as she said, "Where'd you and Hale disappear to last night?"

"Nowhere," Kat said.

"Turn," Gabrielle instructed. Kat moved a half step, but her gaze never left the garden. "Remind me…didn't you used to be a better liar?"

Kat sighed. "Probably."

Even with a straight pin between her teeth, Gabrielle managed to nod and say, "Thought so." She gripped the skirt's hem, then cried, "Ouch!"

Kat glanced down in time to see Gabrielle pulling a stray pin from her finger.

"You don't have to do this, you know," Kat said. "Marcus is working on the costumes."

"The last time Marcus made our costumes, you looked like a nun."

"I *was* a nun."

Gabrielle shrugged as if that were utterly beside the point. "Besides" – Kat heard the teasing tone in her cousin's voice again – "you've got legs."

"Thanks," Kat said flatly.

"What's wrong? Are you afraid your men might notice?"

"What men?"

"You know..." Gabrielle teased. "Your *boyfriends*... Hale and the new kid."

"Hale's not my boyfriend," Kat blurted.

"Of course not." Gabrielle rolled her eyes. "Hale is definitely *not* your boyfriend."

"But you just said—"

"Let's face it, Kitty Kat. Of all the men you've known in your life, Hale's the first guy who *could* be your boyfriend." Kat started to protest, but Gabrielle silenced her with a hand. "And a tiny little part of that great big mind of yours has always thought that someday he *would* be your boyfriend."

Kat wanted to deny it, but she'd forgotten how to speak.

"Turn," Gabrielle commanded, but Kat didn't move. She just watched her cousin finish. "And Nick...well, Nick's the new Hale."

"No" – Kat's voice was as sharp as the pins in Gabrielle's hand – "he's not."

Gabrielle raised her eyebrows. "Well then, maybe you should make sure the old Hale knows that." Kat stood perfectly still for a long time, thinking about the guys in her life: the ones she could trust and the ones she could con, wondering if she really knew the difference – wondering if, in that respect, she'd ever be as wise as Gabrielle.

"Do you like Nick?" Kat asked timidly. "I mean...do you trust him?"

Kat felt her cousin's hands fall away from the skirt. "Those, Kat my dear, are two very different questions. Why do you want to know?"

"Do you remember that day I was late coming back from the Henley – the day before I met Nick? I saw Taccone that afternoon. He gave me these—"

"Excuse me, miss?"

Kat turned to see Marcus in the doorway of the dressing room, holding a massive bouquet of roses and lilies and orchids so rare that Kat imagined they must have been stolen from nature itself.

Gabrielle squealed and ran toward them. "Oooh! Sven!" she cried, reaching for the card. But then she stopped. A shadow seemed to fall across her face. "They're for you."

Her cousin tried to hand her the card, but Kat stood back, staring. Something told her that nothing that beautiful ever came without some kind of string attached, so she didn't reach for the flowers. She didn't want to listen as Gabrielle started to read.

"'I was sorry to hear that your father is currently unavailable. Nevertheless, I am looking forward to seeing you very soon. Yours, A. Taccone.'"

The room was suddenly cold, the smell of the flowers overpowering. Gabrielle seemed like the wisest person in the world as she sighed and said, "Sometimes I really hate boys."

2 DAYS
UNTIL DEADLINE

ROME,
ITALY

TWENTY-NINE

La Casa di Vetro was neither Rome's most expensive restaurant nor its most exclusive, but Kat could see why it was Arturo Taccone's favourite. There were no tourists here, no crowds – only decadent smells and soft candlelight. But as she walked through the intimate dining room, she thought back to the look on Abiram Stein's face as he'd stared at *Two Boys Running Through a Field of Haystacks*, and she remembered that the man at the small secluded table in the corner was evil. It didn't matter that they were in one of the greatest restaurants in the world; he was still a common criminal.

But then again, Kat realized, so was she.

"Hello, Katarina." Taccone smiled as Kat settled into her chair. His eyes passed to Gabrielle, who stood, arms crossed, three feet away. "And who is this?" he asked, appraising the beautiful girl with cold disinterest.

"She's the muscle," Kat answered simply.

Taccone smiled. "I assume you got my flowers." His voice was low against the din of the crowd.

"They were beautiful."

"Well," he said casually, dabbing his napkin to the corner of his mouth, "I do hope they brought you some joy. You have been working so very hard."

"I drink caffeine," she said calmly. "Lots of it. Gives you pep."

Arturo Taccone laughed softly, but there was something odd about the sound. As if it too had been stolen from its rightful owner.

He sliced into a beautiful filet. But as he brought his fork to his mouth, he paused. "Forgive me. Are you sure I can't get you and your companion something?"

"Thank you, but no."

"I must say, you have not made things easy for me, Katarina." He took a bite. "Interesting. But not easy."

"If it makes you feel any better, my own father would probably agree with you."

"Ah, yes." He took a sip of wine. "How is your father? Does prison agree with him? I hear he's coping quite well. Of course, the case against him is…shaky. A single eyewitness, I understand."

"Yes," Kat said. "You're looking at her."

A shocked smile spread across Arturo Taccone's face,

and Kat felt a sense of pride that she had won one round of whatever game they were playing. She only wished the game were over.

"I do hope I'll see you again when this is finished, Katarina. A man in my position has so many uses for a person with your talents."

"I'll keep that in mind," Kat lied, then changed the subject. "I'm not going to tell you when," she told him, "but you'll know when it happens."

"So, clandestine operations are not your forte, then?"

"Maybe. Or maybe I'm just counting on one of the half dozen guys you have stationed outside the Henley to tip you off when the time comes."

He smiled, and Kat knew that this was somehow the highlight of his incredibly decadent dinner.

She reached into her pocket and pulled out a slip of paper. "Twenty-four hours after it's over I'll meet you at this address with the paintings." She stood, and it felt as if a great weight had been lifted from her.

"You're very thorough, Katarina. I meant what I said. When this is finished, you do not have to go back to the Colgan School – or someplace like it. This, as they say, *could* be the start of a beautiful friendship."

Kat looked at her cousin. "I already have all the friends I need."

* * *

The lights were off when they got back. The house was still, peaceful. Sleeping. Or so she thought.

"Hi, Hale."

She saw him through the open door of the dining room, sitting at an ancient-looking table. Twenty high-backed chairs surrounded him, but Hale was alone at the table's head. He was there, Kat knew, waiting for her.

"Hot date?" she asked. But this time Hale didn't have a comeback.

"Are you gonna get mad if I say I don't like you going to see him alone?"

"Jealous?" she said, trying to tease, but the boy in the shadows wasn't smiling.

"Take Angus and Hamish. Take Simon." Kat raised her eyebrows. "OK, so don't take Simon. Take...Nick, if that's what you want." Hale seemed to stumble on the name. "Just don't trust Taccone, Kat."

"I took Gabrielle." Kat pointed at her cousin, who was walking through the front door.

"I was the muscle," Gabrielle called. She didn't break her stride as she started up the stairs.

And yet Hale didn't smile. In fact, it seemed to Kat as if he hadn't even heard. She wondered how many miles

266

they'd logged so far, how many more they had to go. But somehow it had only been thirteen days since they'd stood in Hale's upstate house, and he'd said the words she couldn't forget.

"You're right. Taccone is a whole different kind of bad."

Hale stood and stepped towards her. "Yeah."

"Why are you doing this, Hale?"

"Why do think?"

Kat looked at the ornate room. The gorgeous mouldings, the polished table. The empty chairs. It was in every way the opposite of Uncle Eddie's kitchen, and somehow Kat already knew the answer to her question.

"Hale, this life…" she started slowly, still practically speechless. "This…what we do – what my family does – it looks a lot more glamourous when you choose it."

"So choose it." He handed her another envelope. Smaller this time. Thinner.

"What's this?" she asked.

"That, darling, is my full confession. Dates. Times." Hale leaned against the antique table. "I thought the crane rental receipt was a particularly nice touch." Kat looked at him, speechless. "It's your ticket back into Colgan. If you want it."

"Hale, I…"

But Hale was still moving, shrinking the distance

between them. He seemed impossibly close as he whispered, "And I didn't choose *it*, Kat. I chose you."

Kat stared at the envelope in her hands, maybe because of what it represented – her second chance – or maybe because she didn't know where else to look, what else to do.

"The delivery is set?" Hale asked, and something in his tone told her she didn't have to say anything – anything at all.

"Yeah." She nodded and fell into step beside him. "No turning back now."

"No guts," he said.

She looked at him. "No glory."

"We're in *way* over our heads."

ONE DAY
UNTIL DEADLINE

WYNDHAM MANOR,
ENGLAND

THIRTY

When Katarina Bishop emerged from her room that Monday morning, she wasn't hoping for sun. She wasn't dreading rain. And yet, as she looked out the circular window at the top of the stairs, there was something about the snow that filled her with dread. Her breath fogged the ancient glass, while all around her she heard the sounds of a crew preparing for a hard day's work, and she knew they'd come too far to turn back.

"Kat?" Hamish's voice was higher than usual. The sight of him elbowing Simon as they stood at the bottom of the stairs was disconcerting. The fact that Simon turned and looked at her and dropped a ridiculously expensive electronic gadget made her panic.

"What?" Kat asked.

But the Bagshaws kept gaping, and Simon kept staring, while Hale simply walked into the foyer and leaned against the railing like he'd just made a very large bet against very long odds – and won.

"What?" Kat asked again as she rushed down the stairs, through the foyer, and into the formal dining room.

The boys followed, but no one spoke.

"Are you guys freaking out on me?" she asked, turning on them. "Because today is not the day for freaking out!" She heard her voice rise, felt her hands tingle. *"What is going on?"* she finally yelled when the staring and the silence became too much.

"Now, isn't this role more fun than a nun?" Gabrielle sauntered into the room, casting a sideways glance at the skirt she had personally hemmed.

Hamish nodded. "Kat...you have...*legs.*"

"And boobs," Angus added, staring quite directly at the section of the white blouse that Gabrielle had made a bit too form-fitting for Kat's personal taste.

"Seriously, Kat," Simon said, inching closer, "when did you get boobs?"

Hamish looked at Hale. "The boobs are new," he said as if that point hadn't already been thoroughly made.

"Is that padded?" Simon held out his hand as if to cop an oh-so-scientific feel.

"Hey!" Kat said, slapping his hand away.

"Her dad's gonna get out of prison one of these days, boys," Hale added. Kat thought she saw the faintest smile on his face as he said it, but then again, it was early. And she was stressed. And there were obviously other things on her mind, especially when the kitchen door swung open and Nick walked in, fresh from the shower and completely unfazed by the scene before him.

He didn't stare at Kat. His hands didn't tremble. He didn't fidget or sweat. There was nothing at all about him that looked as if it were anything other than a normal day.

He walked toward her. "Are you ready?" he asked. Was she ready for the biggest job of her life? Was she ready for it to be over? Was she fully prepared to be the only thief in history to ever successfully *remove* something from the Henley without permission? "You've got everything?"

She nodded, grabbed a scone from the tray in Marcus's hand, and started for the door.

"Kat," Hale called after her.

Hamish whispered something that sounded suspiciously like, "What do you think? C-cup?"

Hale pushed into the foyer and caught Kat by the arm, stopping her. "Kat..." he started, but when Nick appeared in the hall behind him, he turned. "You mind?" he said in a tone Kat had never heard him use – not playful but not threatened, and Kat didn't know how to read him.

Nick looked at Kat, who nodded. "Just give me a second."

She heard Nick walk a few feet down the hallway, but her gaze never wavered from Hale's. The Henley and the crew and her father felt a million miles away.

"Kat." He stole a quick glance at Nick, then put his right palm on the wall behind her. She felt the warmth of it on her shoulder as he leaned even closer and whispered, "I have a bad feeling about this."

"It's a little late to stop now, Hale. As you can see, I've already broken out my boobs for the occasion, so—"

"I'm serious, Kat. I don't trust him."

Kat studied the way he looked at her. She found herself reaching out, the tips of her fingers skimming the sides of his starched white shirt.

"Trust me." And with that, Kat slipped away and went outside, felt Nick fall into step beside her. But something made her stop and turn and call, "Ten thirty." Hale nodded but stayed silent, and Kat's heart kept pounding in her chest, loud. Too loud. "I'll see you at ten thirty," she said again.

Hale smiled. "Oh, I'll be there."

THIRTY-ONE

That Monday morning began as Monday mornings at the Henley almost always did. The person responsible for making the coffee made coffee. The person who kept track of birthdays brought cake. The staff briefing ran long as Gregory Wainwright talked about rising attendance levels and falling donations. But on that Monday morning, it seemed that fewer people whispered about Visily Romani than they had the week before. All in all, everyone concluded, it had been a most spectacular November.

Outside, the snow was nothing more than a light powdering, and guards and tourists alike watched it blow across the grounds like chalk dust. Or perhaps it was just the rows and rows of school buses lined up outside the main doors that brought this particular image to mind.

"Field trip season," one of the guards told another.

"Blasted kids," an old man complained.

No one would have ever guessed that seven of the

world's most talented teenagers were coming to the Henley that day for an entirely different sort of lesson.

"What's wrong?" Katarina Bishop asked her dark-haired companion.

Nick stopped and let another long row of school kids pass, while a nearby docent lectured on the importance of light to the great Dutch artists of the eighteenth century.

"Nothing," he said.

He didn't look like the boy who had stood calmly in the kitchen that morning, the con artist who had picked her pocket on a Paris street. Nick seemed different as they walked down the main corridor. Scared? Kat wondered. Nervous? She wasn't sure. But different he was, and as she stopped midstride in the centre of the wide atrium, Hale's warning echoed in her ears.

"If you want out, Nick—"

"I don't want out."

"—you say the word. Right now." She pointed through the glass atrium toward the patchy rays of sunshine and the dry white snow. "You can leave."

"I don't want out." He glanced around the crowded halls. The guards. The docents. The charming older couples with their sketchbooks and packed lunches. Just another day at the Henley. "It's just…busier than I thought it would be."

Kat didn't know if it was nerves or stress or the heat of the sun in that glass room, but the first beads of sweat were starting to appear on Nick's brow. And so she asked herself the simple question: What would her father say? Or Uncle Eddie? Or her mom?

"Busy," she said, citing every great thief she'd ever known, smiling as if she were just another girl and this was just another day, "is very, very good."

Pretend and it will be true. Gabrielle would never know which member of her family had said it first, but that was the thought that filled her mind as she put one foot in front of the other, sashaying through the Henley's largest room.

"This way." Her voice was clear and smooth like the modern sculpture that twirled overhead, catching rays of sunshine and sending them spinning around the grand space. "The Henley's famous promenade was designed by Mrs Henley herself in 1922."

No one in the group of tourists that trailed behind her seemed to notice that her skirt was a little shorter than dictated by the Henley's official handbook. Or that her heels were slightly too high.

"If you'll follow me, I'll show you to the Henley's magnificent Impressionist gallery, which is home to the largest collection of Renoirs in the world. Thanks to a generous contribution from one of our benefactors, we will be able to offer you sole use of this space for the entire afternoon."

The guards who manned the security room that morning were veterans. Collectively, the team assembled behind the bank of monitors had seen almost everything in their day, from couples kissing in lifts to mothers scolding children in dark corners, businessmen who picked their noses when they thought no one was looking, and a very famous movie star who had been caught on camera making a most unfortunate decision about a pair of seemingly uncomfortable underpants.

So when the two workmen from Binder & Sloan Industrial Heating and Air arrived at the service entrance, this same security staff looked at the two young men with a scepticism that comes from years of practice.

"Morning, gents," Angus said as he climbed from the driver's seat of the large van that Hale had secured for that very purpose. "We hear someone's got a" – he made a show of reading from the clipboard in his hand – "faulty Windsor Elite furnace. We're here to fix it."

The guard in charge took a moment to closely examine the two men. They didn't look much older than boys. Their blue overalls seemed to bulge as if they had looked at the snow that morning and put on an extra set of clothes to protect against the chill. Something about the pair was odd, to say the least. But the memo about the faulty furnace had been sent from Gregory Wainwright himself, so the guard saw nothing wrong with pointing towards a large set of double doors and saying, "Furnace is in the basement – right down there."

"Basement?" Hamish cried, then glanced at his brother. "You hear this fellow? He thinks we can just go on down to the furnace and start tinkering?"

Angus laughed. "He probably wouldn't care at all if the whole place went boom, he wouldn't."

At this the guard bristled and stood up even straighter. "Now see here—"

"No, you see, my good man. Out here, see, we've got snow. So in there, I'd bet, you've got heat. And where there's heat there's gas; and where there's gas there's..."

Angus trailed off while his brother said, "Boom."

"So where *do* you need to go?" the guard asked in disgust.

Angus tapped the clipboard in his hand. "First floor. Main corridor."

The guard looked at the Bagshaws one final time. He did not see the boys hold their breath as they waited to hear him say, "Well...all right."

* * *

In such a public place, on such a busy day, it was no surprise at all that no one worried when a smaller-than-average boy with curly hair and a shirt that never stayed tucked in, slipped into the men's room on the second floor. Of course, they also didn't hear the same boy say, "Kat, I'm in position in my...office."

As offices went, sadly, Simon had seen worse. The toilet cubicle was larger than the cupboard he'd been locked inside in Istanbul. The toilet was far more comfortable than the tree stump he'd been forced to use as a desk in Buenos Aires.

He sat perfectly still, waiting for his laptop to start up, and as he looked down at the video image of Gregory Wainwright asleep in his office, Simon had to smile and think that he had been in far worse situations indeed.

Kat had been right fifteen days before when she'd sat in the library of Hale's upstate house and asked if his family owned a mobile phone company. Fifteen days. Somehow, to Hale, it felt longer.

When his phone rang, Hale answered but didn't say hello. He stood outside the Henley, braced against the cold, and listened to Uncle Eddie's gruff "I heard from Paris. You were right about him."

And that was all either of them had to say. Hale slowly slipped the phone back into his pocket and stared at the big glass door.

"Well, are we getting on with this, or aren't we?" Marcus's voice brought Hale back to the moment. "Be mindful of the" – the sound of the thump cut him off midsentence – "bump."

As Katarina Bishop walked down the long hallway towards the Romani Room, she didn't seem to notice the two boys in the blue jumpsuits who were busily working around an open vent and several large machines. She skirted around the temporary barriers and nodded politely at one of the uniformed guards who stood nearby.

The man nodded back and said, "Sorry about the work, miss Can I help you find something?"

"Oh, I don't know." Kat looked at the art-lined hallway as if she were seeing it for the first time. "I'm just…looking, I guess."

"You go ahead and look all you want. But don't touch." The guard chuckled.

And as Kat stepped into the Romani Room, she smiled and thought, Oh, I wouldn't dare.

Sometime in the past week, the Henley's least impressive collection had become Katarina Bishop's favourite. Maybe it was the simple brushstrokes, the subdued use of light. Or maybe Kat was simply drawn to the *other* paintings that hung in that room – the ones the tourists couldn't see.

Collectively, Arturo Taccone's paintings were worth more than half a billion dollars...and her father's life.

"How are we doing, Simon?" she whispered into the small microphone in her collar.

"Just about..." Simon started slowly. And then he stopped. "Wow."

"What?" she asked, panic in her voice.

"Nothing," he said too quickly.

"What?" she asked again.

"Well...it's just that...your boobs look even bigger on TV."

Kat took that opportunity to turn and glare at the nearest security camera. In his cubicle thirty feet away, Simon nearly fell off the toilet.

Kat wanted to look at her watch, but she didn't dare. It was really happening, and there was nothing she could do to reverse it.

The crowd at the mouth of the Romani Room was already parting. Girls were turning to stare at the young billionaire entering the room. And in front of him – in a wheelchair – was Marcus.

"You see him?" Simon said in Kat's ear, and she started to nod, but in that instant, Hale caught Kat's eyes across the room.

They weren't supposed to know each other.

There wasn't supposed to be a look. A word. Not even the smallest glance.

And yet Hale was staring right at her, a desperate look in his eyes.

"Slow down!" Marcus snapped, and Kat wasn't sure whether he was in character or not. He was supposed to be a cantankerous old man, but it was also true that Hale was proceeding far too quickly in her direction. "Let me out of this contraption!" Marcus shouted.

This seemed to remind Hale that there was a larger game at play. He stopped the wheelchair, and Marcus gripped the handrails as if attempting to push himself up.

"Now, Uncle," Hale started, leaning down towards the man who was no more his blood relative than Uncle Eddie, "you know the doctors said—"

"Doctors!" Marcus snapped. It was the single-loudest thing Kat had ever heard him say. The word echoed in the long room. More people were turning to stare. Kat worried that Marcus might be enjoying his moment a bit too much, but there was nothing she could do about it.

"Don't just stand there!" he snapped at Hale in the manner of someone who had several years' worth of snaps bottled up inside of him and was very much enjoying this opportunity to let them out. "Help me up."

He tried to push himself upright, but again Hale was there to discourage him.

"But, Uncle, wouldn't you enjoy the collection more from the comfort of—"

"If you expect me to look at art from that angle, you're as stupid as you are insolent."

A look of complete satisfaction gleamed in Marcus's eyes, and Kat didn't know if he was speaking as Hale's butler or his "Uncle" right then, but it was almost worth the price of everything to see Hale forced to take Marcus's elbow and help him to stand.

"You know, I met Picasso once." Marcus nodded towards a painting. "He was a pompous old—"

"Come this way, Uncle," Hale said, still holding Marcus's arm, but forgetting about the wheelchair and the crowds, the ticking clock and the job. Instead, he seemed to have one purpose as he crossed the room, staring at the girl in the corner.

Stick to the plan, Kat tried to tell him with her eyes.

I need to talk to you, Hale seemed to say.

The crowd was growing thicker. Hale was growing

closer. Kat had the sinking feeling that maybe everything was going to run off track before it even started.

And then a voice cut through the crowd.

"Mr Hale?" Gregory Wainwright's voice was strong and clear. "I *thought* that was you. How do you do, sir?" Mr Wainwright said, turning to Marcus.

Marcus, it seemed, was not quite as prepared to speak to other people as he was to insult Hale. "I...um...I... I loathe women in trousers!"

As Gregory Wainwright studied the man, Kat began to wonder if she might be allowed to share a cell with her father in prison, but then the Henley's director did what people whose careers depend on donations always do: he smiled. And nodded. And said, "Quite right, sir. Quite right indeed."

"Mr Wainwright," Hale said, snapping back into character, "how are you today?" Despite his words, he was still easing toward Kat. The clock was still ticking – too loudly – in her mind.

"Very well indeed, sir. So nice to see you again. And you" – he turned to Marcus – "you must be..."

"Fitzwilliam Hale," Marcus said, reaching up to shake the man's hand. "The...Third," he added at the last second. Hale looked like he wanted to roll his eyes. Kat felt like she wanted to strangle both of them.

"Your nephew was kind enough to tell me about his Monet a few days ago," the curator told Marcus.

"That piece of rubbish!" Marcus snapped.

Again, Hale found her gaze. *I need to talk to you*, he seemed to scream.

Get control of Marcus, she wanted to scream back.

"Now, at my chateau I've got a lovely little Cezanne – Cezanne was a *real* artist," Marcus was saying, and the curator nodded encouragingly; but before the lie could go any further, a screaming siren filled the room.

Kat's first thought was, We're done for.

Her next thought was to glance around the room and see the cloud of dark smoke that was sweeping through the doorway, towards the precious paintings.

She couldn't hear a thing over the wail of the sirens. All she could see through the smoke was the Henley's director grabbing his two VWPs (very wealthy people) and pushing them towards the doors.

Suddenly, guards were everywhere. Docents appeared as if through the walls. Kat was caught in the current – just another body being pushed towards the exits, forced closer to the smoke and the wailing sirens and the even more crowded hall.

Hale turned to look behind him, searching the crowd and finding her one last time. But Gregory Wainwright had a grip on his arm, and Hale was gone with the current, washed away on a wave of fear.

"This way!" the man said, dragging Hale and Marcus along.

"But my chair," Marcus finally remembered to say, but the museum's director didn't hear him; the exhibits were already locking down. And the moment for turning back was long since gone.

THIRTY-TWO

Kat had always heard that if there was one thing the great museums of the world feared more than theft, it was fire. In that moment, she didn't doubt it. The pulsing sirens were even louder than when Gabrielle had lain unconscious on the floor. Children screamed. Tourists ran. People crushed against each other in the smoke and chaos, rushing towards the front doors and the fresh wintry air outside.

And that is probably why the director of the Henley didn't notice the boy who pressed against him, fighting through the crowd. He reached into the man's interior jacket pocket for the small plastic card, freeing him of that particular burden as the crowd pushed on. Then he found his way through the smoky haze to the Romani Room, and the girl who stood waiting.

"Not bad," Kat mouthed as the boy silently swiped the card through the reader. A red light turned green.

The automatic locks were overridden quietly. And Nick smiled and mouthed, "Thanks."

As Kat stepped inside the Romani Room, she smelled the trace of smoke that still hung in the air. She heard the roar of sirens fade behind the massive airtight and fireproof doors as they locked into place. She knew that there was only one way out.

Despite the flashing red emergency lights, the room was beautiful – the glossy floor, the glistening frames, and, of course, the paintings. There were no guards between Kat and those priceless works. No staring docents or tacky tourists.

Kat started to take a step forwards, but a hand caught her arm.

"Not yet," Nick said. He glanced up at the security camera, and Kat remembered the blind spot. She glanced at the floor and thought about the sensors.

She waited.

"Any second now," Simon said through her earpiece.

"*This year* would be good," Nick replied.

"You can't rush greatness, guys," Simon chided back, and Kat thought he sounded a tad too cocky for a boy who was currently operating out of the third toilet cubicle on the left.

Suddenly, the red glow of the emergency lights was replaced by a pulsing blue light. "Simon!" Kat cried. "Rush something!"

A new siren – softer but somehow twice as menacing – sounded, coursing through the room.

"Simon! We've got to move. Now!"

"Just a second," he said.

But Kat didn't care about the encryption that was currently keeping them at bay. She was far more concerned about the spinning blue lights and the mechanical voice that was counting down, saying, "Fire-protection measures will take effect in FIVE. FOUR…"

"Simon!" Kat cried.

"Just one—"

"We don't have a second!" Kat yelled just as the lights stopped spinning and a sound more terrifying than any siren pierced the air.

"Of course it is!" Gregory Wainwright shouted. A mobile was trained to his ear, but his gaze stayed fixed on the two billionaires (or, more accurately, one billionaire and one butler) who stood five feet away, watching dark smoke spiral into a pale grey sky.

The Henley, after all, was burning. And all Gregory Wainwright could do was stand at a safe distance, yelling at the fire.

Hale felt the man staring, recognized the forced authority in his voice as he barked, "Absolutely! You should do that."

Hale turned his back against the cold wind and tried not to think about the smoke, the fire, and most of all...

"Kat," he whispered, silently cursing himself. He should have forced her to talk to him. He should have left Marcus, abandoned his role – made Kat listen to what Uncle Eddie'd had to say. But it was too late. He was stuck outside with the director while she was locked in there. With Nick. And right now Hale was as useless as Wainwright as he stood out in the cold, trying to pinpoint the moment when it all went wrong.

It was a good plan, wasn't it? They had been prepared, hadn't they? Or maybe not. A crew is only as strong as its weakest link, after all. Maybe they had been reckless and stupid and careless. Maybe Uncle Eddie had been right. Maybe this was simply what happened to people who dared to take on Visily Romani.

"Now, now, Mr Hale." The director placed a comforting hand on Hale's shoulder. "There's no need to worry. I assure you, our fire-protection measures are state of the art."

"That is a relief," Hale muttered.

"In fact, that was my head of security on the phone just now," the director said. "He assures me that the affected area was completely evacuated." But then Gregory Wainwright seemed to notice the concern this news brought to Hale's eyes. "Don't worry, Mr Hale. Our fire-protection measures will be activated any second now."

"What kind of measures would those be?" Marcus asked.

The director chuckled. "Well, we can't use your common garden hose, now, can we? The water would do as much harm to a three-hundred-year-old painting as the smoke and fire would. Instead, we simply suck all the oxygen out of the room. Without oxygen, any fire dies."

The director's phone rang again. He turned to take it while Hale's gaze turned back to the museum, his thoughts on the girl still stuck inside, with the boy who would never be a member of the family.

Kat knew the change was coming before she heard the terrible sucking sound.

"Simon…" she said again, fighting the urge to run across the room before she heard Simon yell…

"Now! The cameras are blind. You're clear."

Kat didn't need to be told twice. She felt Nick at her

elbow as they ran side by side down the length of the long exhibit hall to where the wheelchair sat, abandoned.

She fumbled with the straps that held the oxygen tanks to Marcus's chair.

"You've got less than six seconds until you're out of air, guys," Simon warned as Kat tossed a tank toward Nick. *"Four seconds,"* Simon said as the hissing, sucking sound grew louder.

The room had grown darker, the paintings somehow fuzzy. And as the floor began to spin, Kat fell to her knees and marvelled at what an excellent security measure a spinning floor made.

"Kat!" Simon screamed her name.

She heard Nick drop the canister. It smashed against his toe and toppled onto the hard floor.

"The masks!" Simon yelled, and something about the word made her notice the long plastic tubes in her hands – see the strange masks protruding from a pouch on the back of Marcus's chair.

Kat was supposed to be doing something, she was sure, but she suddenly felt so sleepy – the masks seemed so far away.

"Kat!" Simon yelled again. She summoned her last ounce of strength, placed the first mask over her mouth, and drew in the pure oxygen.

The floor stopped spinning.

The paintings suddenly seemed beautiful again.

While Kat surveyed the room, Nick carefully unscrewed pieces of the wheelchair. As he tipped the metal tubes, a variety of tools slid into his palms. They both kept goggles secured over their eyes, and their breathing masks over their mouths, so there was no talking as Nick placed a tool into her hands, and Kat walked to the first painting, *Flowers on a Cool Spring Day*.

In the past week, Kat had come to love the combination of colours in the blossoms, the play of the light. It was not Henley's most prized possession, but Kat found it beautiful in a soothing way. Yet nothing would ever be as beautiful as what Kat hoped lay behind it.

She looked at Nick. Despite the rush of pure oxygen, she felt frozen.

It's back there, she told herself. Almost involuntarily, she reached to touch the place where Visily Romani's business card had mysteriously appeared in the middle of the night ten days before.

Something is back there, her heart seemed to say.

It could be a trap, her mind wouldn't let her forget.

Nick held up his digital watch; the display was bright in the dim room, counting backwards from five minutes.

A physical reminder of what neither of them could afford to forget – they didn't have all day.

As Kat gripped a pair of needle-nose pliers in her hand, she looked at her right arm, expecting to see a tremble, praying her three months at Colgan hadn't taken this from her too – but her gloved hand was steady as it moved to the top of the painting's ornate frame and found the pressure sensor. Nick handed her a piece of Silly Putty, and she pressed it against the small button that she could not see.

Needle-nose pliers and Silly Putty, Kat thought. Ain't technology grand?

Preparing to move the painting from the wall was the easy part. It was as simple as spraying a spritz of air across the back of the frame, double-checking for additional sensors, then reaching for the painting and easing it from the wall.

The hard part was fighting the overwhelming sensation that she might have been wrong; it might have been a goose chase, a prank – the greatest con Visily Romani had ever pulled.

"Kat?" Simon's voice was in her ear. "Hurry it up. Beta team is in position."

But Kat couldn't rush. She could barely breathe as she lifted the frame, peeled back the canvas, and came face-to-face with a ghost, a painting behind the painting. An image that was anything but *Flowers on a Cool Spring Day*.

She'd seen it before, of course. Once on a video feed and once in a picture. But as Nick carefully replaced the other painting in its frame and returned it to the wall, all Kat could do was stare at the two boys who were still running through haystacks, chasing a straw hat and a strong breeze through decades and across a continent.

Nick searched her eyes. Kat watched him mouth the words "What's wrong?" But Kat was thinking about Abiram Stein, whispering even if only for herself, "I know someone who has been looking for this."

THIRTY-THREE

Everything had gone almost exactly according to plan. Or at least that's what the various members of the Henley's security department told themselves.

The entire building had been evacuated in less than four minutes. The fire itself had been contained to a single wing of the Henley's six sections. A hallway, really, located far away from the major exhibits like the Renaissance room and Impressionist gallery. So now the Henley's only fear was minor smoke damage to minor paintings.

If any of the members of the staff had stopped to think about it, they might have wondered how the smoke-to-fire ratio had been so strangely high to begin with, but they didn't. Instead, they patted themselves on the back and looked forward to bonuses and commendations once word of their quick thinking and clear resolve reached the powers that be.

Far away from the Romani Room, locked inside the

Henley's security annexe, they watched the various exhibits through an eerie haze, not noticing that the feed was nothing but a continuous loop; not seeing the Bagshaw brothers and Simon as they made their way down the empty hallways towards a door that was certainly locked – a wing the guards were sure was abandoned.

No one in the guard room saw Simon raise his hand and knock. Not a soul noticed when Gabrielle pushed open the door to the Henley's second best exhibit. She studied the trio and said, "You're late."

The paintings were there.

Kat held them in her gloved hands. She saw them through her goggled eyes. It was not a dream or a mirage – they were there. And yet she couldn't let herself believe it.

"Two and a half minutes," Simon warned as Kat walked past the four frameless canvases that leaned against the wall like the artists' stalls on the streets of New York and Paris. It wasn't hard to imagine that she'd gone back in time a few hundred years and was looking at the works of a few unknowns, guys named Vermeer and Degas.

Nick had taken off his blazer and tie and was now hurrying around the hot room, packing, preparing for the next phase, but one painting remained, and as Kat eased toward it, she could feel the seconds passing, and something else...hope? Fear?

But the feeling that mattered most was the massive whoosh of rushing air that was suddenly cascading through the vents, blowing across Kat's face and through her hair as she reached towards the final painting and then stopped, looked up, and heard a familiar voice say, "Hello, Kitty Kat."

Gabrielle's hair should have been tousled as she hung upside down, dangling from an air duct twenty feet above the ground. Her face should have been smudged. It was one of life's great injustices, in Kat's opinion, that some girls could crawl through two hundred feet of ductwork and come out on the other side looking even more glamorous for the adventure. But the single most remarkable thing about Kat's cousin in that moment was the look on her face as she scanned the row of paintings and whispered, "It's them."

Kat and Nick ripped off their oxygen masks. They tossed their goggles aside. Fresh air was rushing past Gabrielle, filling the gallery, as Kat moved towards the last painting and reached carefully for the pressure switch. Despite the fresh air, Kat held her breath as she eased the final painting from the wall, turned it over, and heard her cousin say, "Uh-oh."

* * *

The scene outside the Henley was exactly what one might expect under these circumstances. Shrill sirens filled the air as fire engines and police cars raced down the cobblestone streets and blocked off a perimeter around the main entrances.

Though the security team swore that the fire had been contained, black smoke still escaped from doors and windows, and then faded into the winter breeze.

The dusty snow had turned to drizzle, so reporters stood under umbrellas as they broadcast the story around the world.

The Henley was burning. And it seemed that all of London had come out to watch the fire.

Gregory Wainwright saw his career dangling by a thread. And yet there was little else he could do while the firemen scrambled off their fire engines and school children huddled together on the pavements for roll call. And so the director maintained his distance from the crowd, standing with the young billionaire and his uncle, making small talk – making allies.

"Well, it was nice seeing you again, Mr Wainwright," Hale said, trying to pull away. "If you'll excuse me, I really must attend to my uncle."

"Oh, dear!" the director exclaimed. "Mr Hale! Forgive me. I completely forgot. Here" – he looked around as if expecting a wheelchair to magically appear out of thin air – "allow me to find you somewhere to rest. Perhaps I can send one of the firemen to retrieve your chair—"

"No!" Hale and Marcus blurted in unison.

"I'm fine," Marcus said again with a dismissive wave of his hand. "I have many just like it. And you have quite enough to worry…" Marcus turned to survey the still-smoking building, the crowds of tourists with their flashing cameras, and the journalists with their plastic smiles. "It does make a man wonder if that Visily Romani business was really nothing after all."

Hale looked at Marcus, but the older man didn't meet his gaze. Instead he tucked his hand into the lapel of his coat in the way he'd seen men of wealth do for the majority of his life. "But I suppose you cannot be blamed if *two disasters* happen within a month."

Hale watched the director's eyes narrow, first with resentment, then puzzlement.

"Coincidences happen," Marcus carried on, but Wainwright was already doing the maths, calculating the odds of a fire and thief coming to the most secure museum in the world within weeks of each other.

"I'm sorry, Mr Hale." The director pulled out his phone and set off at a frantic pace. He paused briefly to call over his shoulder, "Please call my assistant about the Monet!"

And, with that, Gregory Wainwright was gone.

"It's not here," Kat said flatly as she stared at the back of the final frame.

"Kat," Simon said through her earpiece, "I'm hearing chatter on the security frequencies. I think—"

But Kat wasn't listening. She was too busy looking at the place where the final painting was supposed to be… but wasn't.

"*Girl Praying to Saint Nicholas… Girl Praying to Saint Nicholas* was supposed to be there!" Kat looked up, past Nick's worried eyes. She completely ignored her cousin, who dangled gracefully from the vent, manipulating a long wire. Instead, Kat's eyes scanned the room, counting, "One, two, three—"

"Kat!" Nick snapped.

"It's not here," Kat said numbly, still staring at the frame in her hands.

"Kat!" he yelled, and this time she met his gaze.

"It's not here."

Maybe it was a mistake. Maybe Visily Romani had hidden the fifth painting behind a different frame, and it was up to Kat to use her last few seconds to choose one and choose wisely.

"It's not—" Kat started again.

But then she saw it – the small white card that was secured to the back of the frame by a single piece of tape in the very place where *Girl Praying to Saint Nicholas* was supposed to be.

Visily Romani *had* been here.

Visily Romani had done this.

Visily Romani had left a trail, and Kat had followed. She'd been more determined than Uncle Eddie, and braver than her father, and more clever than the cleverest minds at Scotland Yard. She had come so far, and standing there, watching her cousin drag four priceless paintings through the air and into the heating duct, it should have been the proudest moment of her life. But all Kat could do was stare and say, "It's not here."

She traced the raised black letters of the business card.

"Kat." Nick's voice was in her ear. His hand tugged gently on her arm. "Kat, it's time."

Time, the greatest thief of all. So Kat didn't stop to ponder the question of the fifth painting's fate.

Instinct and breeding and a lifetime's worth of training were taking over as Kat ran to the empty hook on the wall and replaced the final frame.

She turned and saw Gabrielle dragging Raphael's *Prodigal Son* by a cable, easing it inside the heating duct just as Simon yelled, "Guys, you are out of time. Get in or—"

"Here!" Nick screamed. He cupped his hands, ready to boost her up to reach the vent, but Kat didn't take his offer.

Instead she reached down and picked up the burgundy blazer and tie where Nick had left them. As she ran her hand over the small, custom-made patch that Gabrielle had hand-sewn over the pocket, she found the words she'd said to Hale coming back to her. "Why are *you* doing this, Nick?"

"Guys!" Simon warned.

"Why, Nick?" she asked, moving closer. "Just tell me… why."

"I… I needed a job."

"No," Kat said simply. She shook her head and, without wasting another second, clutched the blazer to her chest with her left hand and grabbed the wire's end with her right. And suddenly she was flying, rising through the air towards the vent.

Once she was securely inside, she looked back at Nick, standing on the ground beneath her.

"Throw me the cable, Kat," he said, staring up at her with an unwavering gaze, and Kat realized she hadn't seen eyes like that since Paris – since the day Amelia Bennett had come to take Bobby Bishop to jail.

"You look like her, you know?" she said, staring down at him.

"Kat," he said again, harsher now. *"Throw down the cable."*

"I should have seen it sooner. I'm pretty sure *Hale* saw it right away." She laughed, despite the sirens and the pressure and the blood rushing to her head as she peered down. "I guess I've had a lot on my mind."

"Kat, throw down the—"

"Taccone likes to threaten people, did you know that? Typical stuff, really. Innuendos...threatening pictures... And when I looked at the ones of my dad, I saw you in them – in the background. Were you following him, Nick? Is that why you followed me?" Kat asked. She didn't wait for him to answer. "I bet you'd been planning to help your mom catch my dad by getting close to me for a long time."

"Kat!" Gabrielle's voice echoed in the distance. She could hear her cousin struggling with the four priceless paintings as they banged against the thin tin walls of the shaft. But still she didn't move.

"How long has your mom been leading the investigation of my dad, Nick?"

He looked down at the ground and admitted, "A while."

"And so she drags you with her all over the world, and somewhere along the way you got sucked into the family business?" She looked at the boy who might have helped her, or might have betrayed her, but had certainly lied to her. And yet she couldn't help saying, "I knew there was a reason I liked you." She moved farther into the shaft. "Maybe you should try boarding school!"

As she inched deeper into the ductwork, Nick called out, "I thought you were retired!"

And something in his voice, or maybe just the moment, made Kat smile. She turned and leaned out of the vent one final time. "Why are you doing this, Nick?"

"Because…" He paused, searching for words. "Because I like you," he said, but Kat didn't believe him.

At that moment a new siren began to wail – a different, deafening sound.

"Kat," Nick said again, stepping forward, reaching up for help, but in that instant, red laser lights flashed over the grate's opening. The cool blue light of the Romani Room was replaced by a bright red glow. Nick glanced towards the doors as if he could hear the guards coming.

But Kat stared down at him and said, "Wrong answer."

* * *

Kat tried to ignore the sirens that grew louder and louder with each inch. She squinted and crawled through the blackness. Focusing on a small square of light in the distance, Kat crawled closer and closer. Louder and louder the sirens wailed. And as badly as Kat wanted to stop and think about what had just happened, there was no room for thought at that point – no time.

When she finally reached the end, she could see Gabrielle beneath her, ripping off the skirt of her docent's uniform, turning it inside out to reveal a burgundy plaid that matched Kat's own. Simon was helping Hamish with his tie, the brothers' blue jumpsuits now shoved deep into a wastebasket somewhere inside the Henley. And then she glanced down at the blazer in her hand. Nick wouldn't be needing it. Not now. So she left it tucked inside the shaft and lowered herself to the floor through the glow of a whirling red light.

Laser grids were flashing angrily. In the chaotic wash of lights, she could barely make out the paintings on the walls – Renoir. Degas. Monet. She felt dizzy with the thought of being that close to so many masters. But then again, maybe it was just the thick gas being pumped into the room.

She thought of the oxygen mask that she'd left behind, but of course it was too late.

Through blurry eyes she saw the doors swing open, armed guards rushed inside.

"Henley security!" Kat heard the cry over and over, reverberating up and down the halls.

Kat's head felt thick. She had already started to fall.

THIRTY-FOUR

From the backseat of Arturo Taccone's Bentley, the entire world seemed to be falling apart. A small television showed live coverage of a correspondent who stood a mere twenty feet away. Taccone looked between the scene on the screen and the one unfolding in real life, and he wasn't quite certain which showed the real picture.

"Things have taken a dramatic turn here at the Henley today," the correspondent was saying.

"What do you want me to do, boss?" the driver turned and asked.

Arturo Taccone took a last look at the scene, then placed his sunglasses over his eyes. "Drive." His voice was cool and free of emotion; as if another round of his favourite game were finally over. A bystander wouldn't have known if he had won or lost. Arturo Taccone was simply happy to be able to play again another day.

He leaned farther back into the plush seat. "Just drive."

* * *

The first men through the gallery doors that day were seasoned professionals. They had trained with the American FBI and the UK's Scotland Yard. Most were former military. Their equipment was state of the art. The Henley staff took it as a personal insult whenever a great museum got robbed. Some might have said that their extreme security measures were overkill, a waste, but at this particular moment on this particular day, they seemed like a very good idea.

Ten men stood at the gallery's entrance, tasers drawn, gas masks over their faces, as they watched doors swing open up and down the Henley's halls.

Collectively, they represented one of the most highly trained private security forces in the world.

And yet nothing could have prepared them for what they saw.

"Wait," the news correspondent said, and immediately Arturo Taccone turned back to the screen. "We are receiving the first, unconfirmed accounts that the Henley might be secure."

"Stop," Arturo Taccone said, and his driver pulled to the kerb.

* * *

"Kids!" Kat heard one of the guards yell through the haze that filled her mind. "It's a bunch of kids!"

She rolled onto her side and looked up through the fog as a man knelt on one knee and leaned towards her. "It's OK," he told her softly.

"Gas," she mumbled and coughed. "Fire. The museum was on—" A coughing fit cut her off. Someone handed her a mask, and she breathed in fresh air.

There was more coughing around the room. From the corner of her eye she saw Simon holding a mask to his face. He was lying on the ground beside an empty artist's stand, clutching a blank canvas. The guards were busy helping Angus and Hamish to their unsteady feet, so they never saw the smallest of the boys smile behind his mask. But Kat saw.

Lying on the floor that day, Kat saw everything.

"What is this?" Kat knew the voice. She had last seen the man disappearing into the crowd and the smoke, but this time Hale was not beside him. "Who are these children?" Gregory Wainwright demanded of the guards.

The guard pointed to the seal on Simon's burgundy blazer. "Looks like they're from the Knightsbury Institute."

"Why weren't they evacuated?" the director asked of the guards, but didn't wait for an answer. He turned and snapped at the teens. "Why *didn't* you evacuate?"

"We—" Everyone in the room turned to the girl with the long legs and the short skirt who was rising unsteadily to her feet. Two of the guards rushed to take her by the arm and help her to stand. "We had a" – coughing overtook her for a moment, but if Gabrielle was playing her part too fervently, Kat was the only one to think it – "had a class."

She pointed to the bag at her feet. Brushes and paints were strewn across the marble floor where they'd fallen in the chaos. Wooden easels stood in a long line, facing the rows of art. No one stopped to notice that there were five children. Five easels. Four blank canvases. No one was in the mood for counting.

"We were supposed to..." She coughed again. One of the guards placed a hand protectively on her back. "They told us to wait here. They said this exhibit was closed so that we could try to copy those." Gabrielle pointed from the blank canvases on their easels to the Old Masters that lined the walls. "When the sirens sounded, we tried to leave, but the doors were—" She coughed one more time and looked up at the men who surrounded her. Her eyelashes might have batted. Her cheeks might have blushed. A dozen different things might have happened, but the end result was that no one doubted her when she said, "Locked."

Well, almost no one.

"What class? Why didn't I know about any such class?" the director growled at the guards.

The gas was almost completely gone. Kat was breathing more normally. She smoothed the skirt of her uniform, feeling as if her balance had almost completely returned. Two and two were starting to equal four again as she turned and pointed to the sign on the open door, which read: GALLERY CLOSED FOR PRIVATE LECTURE (THIS PROGRAMME MADE POSSIBLE BY THE W. W. HALE FOUNDATION FOR ART EXCELLENCE).

"But..." the director started, then turned. He ran a hand across his sweating face. "But the oxygen? The fire security protocols should have killed them!" He turned back to Gabrielle. "Why aren't you dead?"

"Sir," one of the guards cut in. "The fire was isolated in the next corridor. The oxygen deprivation measures wouldn't have kicked in here unless—"

"Keep searching the galleries!" the director yelled. "Search them all."

"The galleries are all secure, sir," one of the guards assured him.

"We thought *this* gallery was secure!" Wainwright looked down, mumbling something to himself about oversights and liability. "Search them!"

"Sir," one of the guards said softly, stepping closer. Kat savoured the irony as he whispered, "They're just *kids*."

"Sir," Simon said, his voice shaking so violently that Kat believed he was honestly on the verge of tears. "Could I call my mother? I don't feel so good."

And then one of the most brilliant technical experts in the world passed out cold.

The sound that came next was unlike anything Katarina Bishop had ever heard. It wasn't the screech of an alarm. It was anything but the roar of sirens. One of the busiest museums in the world was like a ghost town, echoing. Haunting. And as the guards carried Simon into the grand promenade and its cleaner air, Kat half expected to see the shadow of Visily Romani hovering over them, telling her somehow that she'd done well, but she wasn't finished. Not yet.

Through the Impressionist gallery's open door, Kat watched Gabrielle slowly putting the blank canvases into the large carrying cases. Hamish and Angus hurriedly stuffed paintbrushes into backpacks. Kat moved to comfort Simon, but then she stopped. She listened.

A thud. An echo. A footstep.

She turned just as the man appeared at the end of the promenade. His arms pumped. His feet banged against the tile floor. And the whole world seemed to stop turning as he told them, "She's gone."

The words weren't a cry, and they were far from a whisper. They held no trace of panic or fear. It was more like disbelief. Yes, that was it, Kat decided, although she couldn't tell if it was his or hers.

"Leonardo's *Angel*," the man said again as the party made its way down the centre of the grand promenade. The big double doors to the Renaissance room were standing open. A fireproof, bulletproof Plexiglas barrier still stood, sheltering the *Angel* from harm. Lasers shone red all around. But there was no mistaking that the frame at the centre of it all – the heart of the Henley – stood empty.

"Gone?" Gregory Wainwright stumbled toward the Plexiglas barrier, reaching out for a painting that was no longer there. "She can't be—" the director started, then seemed to finally notice that the frame wasn't empty after all. The *Angel* was gone, but something remained: a plain white card and the words, "Visily Romani".

If they had searched Kat, of course, they would have found a card exactly like it. If they had peeled back the top layer of canvas that covered the four frames Kat's crew carried, they would have seen that *Angel Returning to Heaven* was not the only painting to leave the Henley that day, although somehow Kat imagined that only four walked out the front door.

Leonardo da Vinci's painting was gone. The five children trapped in the mayhem were no longer a top concern. And so it was that Simon, Angus, Hamish, Kat, and her cousin walked out into the fading drizzle with four masterpieces secured in their artist's portfolios, covered with blank canvas – a clean slate.

Kat breathed the fresh air. A clean start.

In the days that followed, no reporters would be able to interview any of the young artists who had been in danger that day. The Henley's trustees waited for a call or visit from one or more attorneys, and word about what monetary damages there might be, but no such call or visit ever occurred.

It seemed to some as if the schoolchildren who had been locked in the Impressionist exhibit that day had simply gathered their bags and blank canvases, and walked out into the autumn air, and faded like smoke.

One of the docents reported seeing the children board a waiting school bus, an older driver at the wheel.

Many people tried in vain to gain a statement from officials at the Knightsbury Institute, but no one could uncover where the school was located – there certainly was no record of any such institution in London. Not in all of England. Some of the children had sounded American, the guards had said, but after three weeks of failed attempts, the coughing children with their hazy eyes were forgotten for a bigger story on another day.

No one saw the man in the Bentley who sat watching them walk from the museum in a single line. No one but he noticed that the portfolios they carried were a tad too thick.

No one but his driver heard him whisper, "Katarina."

THIRTY-FIVE

Gregory Wainwright was not a foolish man. He swore this to his wife and to his therapist. His mother assured him of that fact every Sunday when he visited her for tea. No one who truly knew him thought that he was personally responsible for Henley security – he employed specialists for such things, after all. But the *Angel*...the *Angel* had gone missing. Had disappeared. And so Gregory Wainwright was fairly certain that the powers that be at the Henley would be inclined to disagree.

Perhaps that is why he did not tell a soul that his security card had somehow gone missing in the chaos of the fire. Perhaps that is why he did not say a lot of things.

If it had been another painting, perhaps all might have been forgiven. But the *Angel*? Losing the *Angel* was too much.

The article that appeared in the evening edition of the London *Times* was not exactly what the public had expected. Of course, the colour picture of the lost Leonardo loomed large in the centre of the page. It went without saying that a headline about the robbery at the Henley dominated everything above the fold. And it was only a matter of time, Gregory Wainwright knew, before the old stories about the *Angel* would resurface. His only surprise was that it had taken less than twenty-four hours for the press to turn the story from a recounting of the Henley's – and society's – loss, to a retelling of the Henley's shame.

It wasn't Wainwright's fault that Veronica Miles Henley had purchased the *Angel* soon after the end of World War II. Wainwright hadn't taken the painting from its original owner and offered it to a high-ranking banking official who had been of great service to the Nazi party. Gregory Wainwright wasn't the judge who had ruled that, since the *Angel* had been purchased in good faith from the banking official's estate, and since it would hang in a public exhibit, it should not be forcibly removed from the museum's walls.

None of this was my fault! the man wanted to scream. But, of course, screaming simply is not done. Or so his mother told him.

The press was loving all of it. The Henley was being villified, and Romani was being made out as some sort of hero – a Robin Hood who headed a merry band of thieves.

Still, if there was one thing that Gregory Wainwright could be grateful for, it was that the journalists never heard about the boy.

Wainwright remembered every detail of that day as if he were reliving it over and over again…

"Our guards assure me that the room in which you were found had been completely evacuated prior to the fire-protection procedures taking effect," Gregory Wainwright said as he sat across from the young man with the dark hair and blue eyes, in the small interrogation room of Scotland Yard. The detectives had assured him that they were too concerned with tracking down the real thief to take much time with the boy; but the Henley's director had felt otherwise.

"I'm not going to sue," was the boy's only answer.

"How exactly did you get into that exhibit?" the man asked again.

"I told you. I told the guy before you. I told the guys before him, and all the way back to the guys who found me, I was in the exhibit when the sirens sounded. I tripped on my way to the door. By the time I got up, I was locked in."

"But I was in that room. I personally can attest to the fact that our doors only lock when a room has been evacuated."

The boy shrugged. "Maybe you've got a security problem." This was, if anything, an understatement, but Mr Wainwright was not in the mood to say so. "Maybe my mom can help you with that," the boy offered. "She's real good at that stuff. You know she works for Interpol."

The woman at the boy's side was attractive and well dressed, Gregory Wainwright could see. He had, after all, an eye for framing people; so many of them walked through the Henley's doors every day. He knew tourists and collectors, critics and snobs, but he could not truly grasp the woman in front of him.

"How did you survive the oxygen deprivation measures?" the director asked, and the boy shrugged.

"Some old dude left his wheelchair. He must have breathing problems, because there was oxygen on the back."

Gregory Wainwright winced slightly as one of the richest men in the world was referred to as "some old dude", but he said nothing.

The woman began to stand. "I understand if there are waivers or documents which you will need us to sign, but I can assure you, you have no grounds to hold my son, and he's been through quite an ordeal."

"I'm afraid your son cannot go anywhere until he has been cleared of—"

"Cleared?" the boy snapped. Gregory Wainwright could not be sure if it was indignation or fear, but there was no mistaking the edge in his tone.

"I was under the impression that the robbery took place in a different wing of the museum," the mother said.

The boy held his arms out wide. "Search me. Go ahead. Just tell me this: exactly what did I take?" His mother placed a calming hand on her son's shoulder, but her look at Wainwright seemed to say that *that* was an excellent question.

"We have no interest in prolonging this matter, Mr Wainwright," the woman said coolly. "I'm sure you have many things to do today. If I could offer some advice, I'd remind you that in matters such as these, time is essential. If you don't recover her within one week, you will likely never do so."

"I know," the director said, pressing his thin lips together in a tight line.

"And, of course, even if she is recovered, fifteenth-century paintings do not do well when they are shoved into duffel bags or thrown into the boots of cars."

"I know," the director said again.

"And I'm sure I do not need to tell you that what happened to my son today was no accident?"

For the first time, it seemed as if the woman held his

full attention. The man gaped, looking from mother to son as if he didn't have a clue what to say.

"Someone planned that fire, Mr Wainwright," she said, and then laughed a very soft laugh. "But I feel silly telling you this." Her dark red lips curled into a soft smile. "I'm sure you probably already know that it was nothing more than a massive diversion." She held one elegant palm over the other. "A sleight of hand."

The museum director blinked. He felt somehow as if he too were still trapped in the oxygen deprivation chamber while a fire raged outside the door. Amelia Bennett stood to her full height and gestured for her son to join her.

"I'm sure a man like you must already know that my son is as much a victim of Visily Romani as you are."

And with that, the final child who had been locked in the Henley that day turned and walked out the door – vanished without a trace.

And Gregory Wainwright was able to go about his nervous breakdown in peace.

DAY OF
THE DEADLINE

PARIS,
FRANCE

THIRTY-SIX

Twenty-four hours after the robbery at the Henley, it was raining in Paris. Arturo Taccone's French driver pulled his limo (a classic Mercedes, this time in dark blue) to the side of the road and allowed the man to stare out at the narrow street lined with small shops. He was not prepared for the tap on the foggy window or the sight of a girl who was too small and too tired for her age crawling into the backseat beside him.

She shook her short hair slightly, and water splashed across the tan leather seats, but Arturo Taccone did not mind. He had too many other emotions right then, and the largest of which – he scarcely dared to admit – was regret that it was over.

"I have heard that cats don't like the rain," he said, gesturing to her frizzy hair and drenched raincoat. "I can see that it is so."

"I've been in worse," she said, and he didn't doubt it.

"I'm very glad to see you, Katarina. Alive and well."

"Because you were afraid I had been burned alive at the Henley, or because you were afraid I might get caught and use our arrangement as a bargaining chip?"

"Both," the man conceded.

"Or were you most concerned that I might take your paintings and disappear myself? That they might go underground for another half century or so?"

He studied her anew. It was rare to find someone who was both so young and so wise, both so fresh and so jaded. "I admit I have been hoping that you might have brought me, shall we say, a bonus? I would pay handsomely for the *Angel*. She would fit in my collection very nicely."

"I didn't take the da Vinci," she said flatly. Taccone laughed.

"And your father did not take my paintings," he said, indulging her, still unwilling to believe. "You do, indeed, have a most interesting family. And you, Katarina, are a most exceptional girl."

She felt it was her turn to return the compliment, but there were some lies that even Uncle Eddie's great-niece couldn't tell. So instead she just asked, "My father?"

Taccone shrugged. "His debt to me is forgiven. It has been most" – he considered his words – "enjoyable.

Perhaps he will steal something from me again sometime."

"He didn't—" Kat started, but then thought better of it.

Taccone nodded. "Yes, Katarina, let us not leave things with a lie."

Kat looked at him as if to measure what amount of truth might lie in the soul of a man like Arturo Taccone, if any soul at all remained.

"The paintings are in pristine condition. Not even a fleck of paint is out of order."

Taccone adjusted his leather gloves. "I expected nothing less of you."

"They are ready to go home." Her voice cracked, and Taccone knew somehow that she wasn't lying – there was a sincere longing in her words. "They're across the street," she told him. "An abandoned apartment." She pointed through the foggy windows. "There," she said. "The one next to that gallery."

Taccone followed her gaze. "I see."

"We're finished," she reminded him.

He studied her. "We don't have to be. As I said before, a man in my position could make a young woman like yourself richer than her wildest dreams."

Kat eased towards the door. "I know rich, Mr Taccone. I think I'll just aim for happy."

He chuckled and watched her go. She was already out of the car when he said, "Goodbye, Katarina. Until we meet again."

Kat stood beneath the awning of a shop and watched him leave the car and cross the street. The driver did not go with him. He walked through the apartment door alone.

Although she was not there to see it, she knew exactly what he found. Five priceless pieces of art.

Four paintings: one of Degas's dancers and Raphael's prodigal son; Renoir's two boys; *The Philosopher* by Vermeer. And something else he hadn't been expecting: a statue that had recently been stolen from the gallery next door.

Kat often wondered what he must have thought as he looked through the dusty, abandoned apartment at the paintings that he loved and then at a small statue that he had never seen before.

She wondered if he turned and watched the door. Perhaps he heard the Interpol officers as they rushed down the wet street and stood poised outside the apartment windows.

Did Arturo Taccone know what was going to happen? Kat would never know. It was enough for her to stand in the damp air and watch the uniformed officials swarm into the place where she had put Taccone's paintings, and her father had stashed his stolen sculpture.

It was very much enough to stand there and watch as Arturo Taccone's driver sped away, which was just as well. Interpol was more than willing to give his boss a ride.

"Are they in there?"

Kat shouldn't have been surprised to hear the voice, and yet she couldn't fight the shock in seeing the boy.

"What do you think?" she asked.

Nick smiled. "I'm not in prison, by the way," he told her. "Just in case you were wondering."

"I wasn't." For a moment he looked almost hurt, so Kat added, "No one arrests a cop's kid for being in a room where nothing was stolen."

But something *was* stolen at the Henley. They stood there for a long time, not talking, until Nick finally said, "He used us...or, I guess...you. This Romani guy used you for a diversion, didn't he?" Kat didn't answer. She didn't have to. Nick stepped closer. "A con within a con." He looked at her. "Are you angry?"

Kat thought about the *Angel* of the Henley, who was, at that moment, probably winging her way back to her rightful home, and she couldn't help herself. She shook her head. "No."

And still nothing could have surprised her more than when Nick smiled and said, "Me neither."

"Are you flirting with me?" Kat blurted.

Kat thought it a valid, scientific question until Nick inched closer and said, "Yes."

She stepped away from him – from the flirting. "Why'd you do it, Nick? And why don't you tell me the truth this time?"

"I thought you'd help me catch your dad at first."

"And then..." Kat prompted.

Nick shrugged and kicked at a pebble on the pavement. It skidded into a puddle, but she didn't hear the splash. "I wanted to impress my mom. And then..."

"Yes?"

"And then I thought I could catch you – stop a robbery of the Henley, be a hero. But..."

Kat stared into the rainy street. She shivered. "I don't take things that don't belong to me."

Nick gestured across the street to the pair of officers who were leading Arturo Taccone from the apartment in handcuffs. "You took from him."

She thought of Mr Stein. "They don't belong to him either."

A moment later another car pulled through the crowd that was quickly growing across the street. A beautiful black-haired woman stepped from the backseat. If she saw her son beneath the awning, she did not wave or smile or question why he'd ignored her instructions not to leave their hotel without permission.

"You really are good, Kat," he told her.

"Do you mean good as in skilled or just…good?"

He smiled. "You know what I mean."

Kat watched Nick walk away, until the police car carrying Arturo Taccone pulled out into the street, blocking her view. As far as she knew, Nick never looked back. Which wasn't fair, Kat thought. Because, from that point on, she was going to be looking over her shoulder for the rest of her life.

Kat sensed more than saw the black limo that pulled slowly to the kerb beside her. She heard a smooth whirling sound as the dark glass of the back window disappeared and a young man leaned out.

"So that fella there is the one who robbed that nice gallery?" Hale asked, his eyes wide as he pointed to the disappearing police car.

"It appears so," Kat said. "I heard he actually slid the statue through a hole in the wall and into that vacant apartment."

"Genius," Hale said with a tad too much enthusiasm.

Kat laughed as Hale opened the door, and she slid

inside. "Yes," she said slowly. "In theory. Except robbing a gallery tends to make the police spend a lot of time *at* the gallery..."

"And then how does a guy get his statue?"

Kat knew it was her turn – her line. But she was tired of playing games. And maybe Hale was too. Maybe.

He glanced down the street where Nick had disappeared. "You're not leaving with your boyfriend?"

Kat eased her head back onto the soft leather. "Maybe." She closed her eyes and thought that perhaps this flirting thing wasn't so difficult after all. "Maybe not... Wyndham?"

She heard Hale laugh softly then call, "Marcus, take us home."

As they eased into traffic, she let the warmth of the car wash over her. She didn't protest as Hale slid his arm around her and pulled her to rest against his chest. It was somehow softer there than she remembered.

"Welcome back, Kat," he told her as she drifted off to sleep. "Welcome back."

Don't miss the next thrilling

HEIST SOCIETY

adventure, *Uncommon Criminals.*

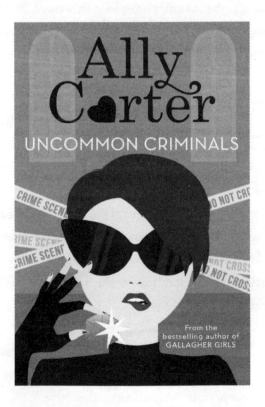

Turn over for a sneak peek!

Moscow can be a cold, hard place in winter. But the big old house on Tverskoy Boulevard had always seemed immune to these particular facts, the way that it had seemed immune to many things throughout the years.

When breadlines filled the streets during the reign of the czars, the big house had caviar. When the rest of Russia stood shaking in the Siberian winds, that house had fires and gaslight in every room. And when the Second World War was over and places like Leningrad and Berlin were nothing but rubble and crumbling walls, the residents of the big house on Tverskoy Boulevard only had to take up a hammer and drive a single nail—to hang a painting on the landing at the top of the stairs—to mark the end of a long war.

The canvas was small, perhaps only eight by ten inches. The brushstrokes were light but meticulous. And the subject, the countryside near Provence, was once a favorite of an artist named Cézanne.

No one in the house spoke of how the painting had come to be there. Not a single member of the staff ever asked the man of the house, a high-ranking Soviet official, to talk about the canvas or the war or whatever services he may have performed in battle or beyond to earn such a lavish prize. The house on Tverskoy Boulevard was not one for stories, everybody knew. And besides, the war was over. The Nazis had lost. And to the victors went the spoils.

Or, as the case may be, the paintings.

Eventually, the wallpaper faded, and soon few people actually remembered the man who had brought the painting home from the newly liberated East Germany. None of the neighbors dared to whisper the letters *K-G-B*. Of the old Socialists and new socialites who flooded through the open doors for parties, not one ever dared to mention the Russian mob.

And still the painting stayed hanging, the music kept playing, and the party itself seemed to last—echoing out onto the street, fading into the frigid air of the night.

The party on the first Friday of February was a fundraiser—though for what cause or foundation, no one really knew. It didn't matter. The same people were invited. The same chef was preparing the same food. The men stood smoking the same cigars and drinking the same vodka. And, of course, the same painting still hung at the top of the stairs, looking down on the partygoers below.

But one of the partygoers was not, actually, the same.

When she gave the man at the door a name from the list, her Russian bore a slight accent. When she handed her coat to a maid, no one seemed to notice that it was far too light for someone who had spent too long in Moscow's winter. She was too short; her black hair framed a face that was in every way too young. The women watched her pass, eyeing the competition. The men hardly noticed her at all as she nibbled and sipped and waited until the hour grew late and the people became tipsy. When that time finally came, not one soul watched as the girl with the soft pale skin climbed the stairs and slipped the small painting from the nail that held it. She walked to the window.

And jumped.

And neither the house on Tverskoy Boulevard nor any of its occupants ever saw the girl or the painting again.

No one visits Moscow in February just for fun.

Perhaps that is why the customs agent looked so curiously at the shorter-than-average teenage girl who stood in line behind the business people and expatriates who were arriving in New York that day, choosing to flee the Russian winter.

"How long was your visit?" the agent asked.

"Three days," was the girl's reply.

"Do you have anything to declare?" The customs agent lowered her head, studied the girl from over the top of her half-moon glasses. "Are you bringing anything home with you, sweetie?"

The girl seemed to consider this, then shook her head. "No."

When the woman asked, "Are you traveling by yourself?" she sounded less like a government official doing her due diligence and more like a mother concerned that such a young girl could be traveling the world alone.

But the girl seemed perfectly at ease as she smiled and said, "Yes."

"And were you traveling for business or for pleasure?" the woman asked, looking from the pale blue customs form to the girl's bright blue eyes.

"Pleasure," the young girl said. She reached for her passport. "I had to go to a party."

Even though she'd just landed in New York, when Katarina Bishop walked through the airport that Saturday afternoon, her mind couldn't help but drift to all the places she still had to go.

There was a Klimt in Cairo, a very nice Rembrandt rumored to be hidden in a cave in the Swiss Alps, and a statue by Bartolini last seen somewhere on the outskirts of Buenos Aires. Altogether, there were at least a half dozen jobs that could come next, and Kat's thoughts wandered through them like a maze. And still the part that weighed heaviest on her were the jobs she didn't know about—the plundered treasures no one had found yet. The Nazis had needed an army, she told herself, to steal them all. But she was just one girl—one thief. She felt exhausted, remembering it might take a lifetime to steal them all back.

When she stepped onto the long escalator and began her descent, Kat was completely unaware of the tall boy with the broad shoulders behind her until she felt the weight of her bag rise gently off her shoulder. She turned and looked up, but didn't smile.

"You'd better not be trying to steal that," she said.

The boy shrugged and reached for the small rolling suitcase at her feet. "I wouldn't dare."

"Because I'm an excellent yeller."

"I don't doubt it."

"And fighter. My cousin gave me this nail file...the thing's just like a switchblade."

The boy nodded slowly. "I'll keep that in mind."

When they reached the bottom of the escalator, Kat stepped onto the smooth floor and realized how insane—

and incredibly sloppy—it was for her not to have seen the boy that every other woman in the terminal was openly staring at. It wasn't because he was handsome (though he was); it wasn't because he was wealthy (though that too was undeniable); there was simply something about W. W. Hale the Fifth—a confidence that Kat knew could not be bought (and almost certainly could never be stolen).

So she let him carry her bags. She didn't protest when he walked so close that her shoulder brushed against the arm of his heavy wool coat. And yet, beyond that, they did not touch. He didn't even look at her as he said, "I would have sent the jet."

"See"—she glanced up at him—"I'm trying to build up the miles."

"Oh, well, when you put it that way..." A split second later, Kat saw her passport appear in Hale's hands as if by magic. "So, how was Moscow, Ms. . . . McMurray." He eyed her. "You don't look like a Sue."

"Moscow was cold," Kat answered.

He flipped the page of the passport and examined the stamps. "And Rio?"

"Hot."

"And—"

"I thought my dad and Uncle Eddie summoned you to Uruguay?" She stopped suddenly.

"Paraguay," he corrected. "And it was more *invitation* than summons. I regretfully declined. Besides, I really wanted to do a Smash and Grab job in a mansion with half the former KGB." He gave a long sigh. "Too bad I never got that invitation."

Kat looked at him. "It was more like a *Gab* and Grab."

"That's too bad." Hale smiled, but Kat felt very little warmth in the gesture. "You know, I've been told that I can really wear a tuxedo."

Kat did know. She'd actually been there when her cousin Gabrielle had told him. But tuxedos, Kat knew, weren't really the issue.

"It was an easy job, Hale." Kat remembered the cold wind in her hair as she'd stood in the open window. She thought about the empty nail that had probably gone unnoticed until morning, and she had to laugh. "Totally easy. You would have been bored."

"Yeah," he said. "Because *easy* and *boring* are two words I frequently associate with the KGB."

"I was fine, Hale." She reached for him. "I'm serious. It was a one-person job. If I'd needed help I would have called, but—" "I guess you just didn't need the help."

"The family is in Uruguay."

"Paraguay," he corrected.

"The family is in *Paraguay*," Kat said louder, but then

she felt herself go quiet. "I thought you were with the family."

He stepped toward her, reached out, and slid the passport into her jacket pocket, just above her heart. "I'd hate to see you lose this."

When he started outside, Kat watched the big glass doors slide open. She braced herself against the freezing wind, but Hale seemed immune to the cold as he turned and called behind him, "So—a Cézanne, huh?"

She held two fingers inches apart. "Just a little one… Weatherby?" she guessed, but Hale merely laughed as a long black car pulled to the curb. "Wendell?" Kat guessed again, hurrying to catch up. She slid between the boy and the car, and standing there, with his face inches from hers, the truth about what the *W*'s in his name stood for didn't seem to matter at all. The reasons she'd been working all winter were blowing away with the breeze.

Hale's *here*.

But then he inched closer—to her and to a line that couldn't be uncrossed—and Kat felt her heart change rhythms.

"Excuse me," a deep voice said. "Miss, excuse me."

It took a moment for Kat to actually hear the words, to step back far enough to allow the man to reach for the door. He had gray hair, gray eyes, and a gray wool overcoat, and the effect, Kat thought, was that he was part butler, part driver, and part literal man of steel.

"You missed me, didn't you, Marcus?" she asked as he took her bags and carried them to the open trunk with a graceful ease.

"Indeed," he said in a thick British accent, the origin of which Kat had long ago stopped trying to pinpoint. Then, with a tip of his hat, he finished, "Welcome home, miss."

"Yeah, Kat," Hale said slowly. "Welcome home."

The car, no doubt, was warm. The roads to Uncle Eddie's brownstone or Hale's country house were all free from snow and ice, and the two of them might have been settled someplace dry and safe within the hour.

But Marcus's hand lingered on the door handle a second too long. Kat's fifteen years as Uncle Eddie's great-niece and Bobby Bishop's daughter had left her senses a bit too sharp. And the wind was blowing in just the right direction, perfectly calibrated to carry the word on the air as a voice screamed, "Katarina!"

In all of Kat's life, only three people routinely called her by her full first name. One had a voice that was deep and gruff, and he was currently giving orders in Paraguay. Or Uruguay. One had a voice that was soft and kind and he was in Warsaw, examining a long-lost Cézanne, preparing plans to take it home. But it was the last voice that Kat feared as she spun away from the car, because the last voice, let's face it, belonged to the man who most likely wanted to kill her.

Kat stared down the long line of taxis picking up fares, travelers hugging and saying hello. She waited. She watched. But none of those three people came into view.

"Katarina?"

There was a woman walking toward her. She had white hair and kind eyes and wore a long tweed coat and a hand-knit scarf wrapped around her neck. The young man at her side kept his arm around the woman's shoulders, and the two of them moved slowly—as if Kat were made out of smoke and she might float away on the breeze.

"Are you *the* Katarina Bishop?" the woman asked, eyes wide. "Are you the girl who robbed the Henley?"

If a person wanted to be technical about it, Katarina Bishop did not rob the Henley—nor did any member of her crew. She was simply one of a group of teenagers who had walked into the most secure museum in the world a few months before and removed from its walls four paintings that were not the Henley's property. The paintings appeared on no insurance statements. They were never listed in any catalogs. The Henley had never paid a dime for any of those works, so even as Kat herself carried one (a Rembrandt) out the museum's doors, she was not breaking a single law. (A technicality verified by Uncle Marco—a member of the family who had once spent eighteen months impersonating a federal judge somewhere in Minnesota.)

So it was with absolutely no hesitation that Kat looked at the woman and said, "I'm sorry. You've been misinformed."

"*You're* Katarina Bishop?" the woman's companion asked, and although Kat had never met him before, it was a question and a tone she had heard a lot since last December.

The girl who'd planned the job at the Henley should have been taller, the question seemed to say. She should have been older, wiser, stronger, faster, and just in general *more* than the short girl who stood before them.

"*The* Katarina Bishop..." The man paused, searching for words, then whispered, "The thief?"

That, as it turned out, was not an easy question to answer. After all, stealing—even for noble and worthy causes—was illegal. Furthermore, if their accents were to be believed, they were *English* strangers, and England was home to the Henley, the Henley's trustees, and, perhaps most important, the Henley's insurance company.

But the primary reason Kat couldn't—or didn't— answer was that she no longer considered herself a thief.

Kat was more of a return artist, a repossession specialist. A highly uncommon criminal. After all, the statue she'd swiped in Rio rightfully belonged to a woman whose grandparents had died in Auschwitz. The painting from Moscow would soon be winging its way toward a ninety-year-old man in Tel Aviv.

So no, Katarina Bishop was not a thief, and that was why she said, "I'm afraid you have the wrong person," and turned back to Hale and the long black limousine.

"We need your help." The woman moved toward her.

"I'm sorry," Kat said.

"We were led to believe that you were quite talented."

"Talent is overrated," was Kat's reply.

She stepped closer to the car, but the woman reached for her arm. "We can pay!"

At this, Kat had to stop.

"I'm afraid you *really* have the wrong person."

With one look from Kat, Hale reached for the limo door. Kat was halfway inside when the woman called, "He said you…help people." Her voice cracked, and the young man tightened his grip around her shoulders.

"Grandmother, let's go. We shouldn't have believed him."

"Who?" The word was sharper than she'd intended, but Kat couldn't help herself. She climbed from the car.

"Who told you my name? Someone said where you could find me, who was it?"

"A man…" the woman muttered, fumbling for words. "He was very convincing. He said—"

"What was his name?" Hale stepped closer to the young man, who had maybe eight years and two inches on him.

"He came to our flat…" the man started, but the woman's whisper was all that Kat could hear.

"Romani." She drew a deep breath. "He said his name was Visily Romani."

Perhaps you have never heard the name Visily Romani. Until two separate cards bearing that name appeared at the Henley four months before, very few people ever had. Kat had never heard those words until that time, but Kat was still a very young person in a very old world. Since then, Kat herself would say, she'd got much, much older.

At least that was how she felt an hour later as she sat beside Hale in a small quiet diner not far from Uncle Eddie's brownstone on the Brooklyn side of the bridge. The old woman and her companion sat on the other side of the booth. Wordless and worn, both looking as if they'd travelled a long, long way to get there.

The place was nearly empty, and yet the young man kept looking over his shoulder at the waitress wiping down tables and the college girl who sat by the window wearing headphones and studying a book on constitutional law. He took the room in with sharp brown eyes behind horn-rimmed glasses.

When he asked, "Are you sure we shouldn't go someplace more private?" he actually sounded afraid.

"This is private enough," Hale answered.

"But—" the guy started, but then Kat placed her elbows on the table.

"Who are you and why are you looking for me?"

"My name is Constance Miller, Miss Bishop," the white-haired woman said. "Or, may I call you by your given name? I feel as if I know you – you and Mr Hale." She smiled at Hale. "Such a lovely young couple." Kat shifted on her seat, but the old woman went on. "I've become something of a fan." She sounded almost giddy, as if her whole life had been comprised of bake sales and Agatha Christie novels, and now she found herself inside the latter.

"I mean to say," the woman went on, "that there's something I would like for you to steal."

Heist SOCIETY

Questions and Answers with Ally Carter

Where did the idea for *Heist Society* come from?

I was in my car, listening to an audiobook. There was a line in the book — something like "I felt like a cat burglar in my own house", and I immediately knew I wanted to write a story about a girl named Kat who was a burglar.

How did you come up with the title?

It was a title that just popped into my head pretty early on, but we (my editor, agent, writer friends) all kept thinking that maybe there was something better. Months and months we searched. We probably came up with dozens of titles — all of which felt wrong. It took a while to realise that was because *Heist Society* was right. Now I can't imagine calling the book anything else.

Who is your favourite character in *Heist Society*?

That's a hard one. I love them all in different ways. Kat is very independent and savvy about some things — not so much others. Her cousin, Gabrielle, is the only other main female character and she's very upfront and honest in a wonderfully blunt and refreshing kind of way.

And then there are the boys... Sigh. So many boys.

Who is more like you, Kat or Cammie (from the *Gallagher Girls* series)?

Well, I'm neither spy nor thief, but I'm sure part of me is in both of them. Kat grew up in a male-dominated world and she's used to being the only girl in the room. That is something from my life/world that I absolutely brought to Kat's character.

What's it like writing two series at the same time?

It can be kinda crazy — especially when you have to switch back and forth between the two. But it's also very fun. I get to spend time with two smart, confident, and highly-skilled characters and in their colourful worlds. I know how lucky that makes me.

BKMRK

Find your place

Want to be the first to hear
about the best new teen and YA reads?

Want exclusive content, offers
and competitions?

Want to chat about books with people
who love them as much as you do?

Look no further . . .

bkmrk.co.uk

 @TeamBkmrk /TeamBkmrk

@TeamBkmrk TeamBkmrk

See you there!